THE HOTEL PENN

Books by L.L. Abbott

Lake Pines Mystery Series
Murder On The Water
Death At Deception Bay
Murder Of Crows
The Dead Of Winter

Anna Ledin Thriller Series
The Blackwater Operative
The Phoenix Code
Rogue
Blown

Teen & Young Adult
Unfollowed
A Hero Among Them
Carole And The Secret Queen's Scarf

Genre Fiction
The Hotel Penn

THE HOTEL PENN

A Novel

L.L. ABBOTT

Cover designed by L.L. Abbott

L.L. Abbott
Visit my website at www.llabbott.com

Paperback ISBN: 978-1-989325-07-0
eBook ISBN: 978-1-989325-06-3
Hardcover ISBN: 978-1-989325-24-7
Large Print Paperback ISBN: 978-1-989325-25-4

For travelers, dreamers, and trailblazers who paved the way for others who followed.

~ especially for Drew, my travel partner

THE HOTEL PENN

*"Life is service – the one who progresses is the
one who gives his fellow men a little more
– a little better service."*
– Ellsworth M. Statler

1

New York City, May 10th, 1993

A ndrew knew when he stepped into the hotel, that what he had to do here today would probably end his career. The rain pounded the windows relentlessly on the west side of the building and the old, cracked seal was weakening under the weeklong assault of storms that pummeled the city. Water ran freely down the edges of the frail window frames and pooled along the moldy edges of the ledge. The windows were the least of the neglected maintenance needs of the hotel that fell into disrepair slowly over the last number of decades. Truth be told, Andrew would never have even considered staying here if he ever needed to book a hotel room in New York. Growing up across from Central Park made him more favorably predisposed to the hotels north of 42nd. And when he returned to visit his grandparents, he chose to stay closer to where they lived on 85th, citing it more of a convenience for him. His grandparents often tried to encourage, well more like coerce him, into staying at The Hotel Pennsylvania because of their emotional attachment to the hotel. He knew it was where they had met and where they both worked when it first opened in 1919. He didn't have the heart to explain the real reason he didn't want to stay there and was astonished he was able to be convinced to be here today.

The crowded room was filled with the dampness of rain-sodden coats and shoes that, after many years, soaked and weighed down the threadbare carpet with a sour odor. Bare light bulbs cast a yellow glow from their mount high above the windows. That is, through the fixtures that even had working bulbs. The room was old, worn, and at the same time, full of hidden secrets and stories. And Andrew became more uneasy with each passing moment.

Along with Andrew, seven other wealthy financiers were present at the community engagement meeting, and if it wasn't for the directives of his grandmother, he would have been present with the same purpose that they were here with today. Andrew pulled off his glasses, still partially fogged with the humidity that hung in the now defunct ballroom, and wiped them clean with the corner of his sleeve. He pinched the bridge of his nose and stretched his eyebrows in an unsuccessful attempt at clearing his nose of the dampness that was threatening a sneeze. Once he felt he averted a burst, he returned his glasses to his face.

A loud crack of thunder reverberated through the room and shook the single pane glass of the windows just as Norman Martindale took his place behind the podium at the front of the room and tried to silence the crowd.

"People, please!" Norman shouted above both the incessant chatter inside and the rumbling thunder outside, "People, please! Take a seat so we can begin!"

Norman Martindale was the youngest son of a prosperous Manhattan lawyer who found his calling at the age of nineteen in the depths and despair of run-down landmarks in and around New York City. He most recently worked tirelessly to save the Cartwright Building from being demolished after digging out evidence that three presidents had stayed there during their time in office. After garnering much acclaim with his many projects, he was a greatly sought-after figure for anyone looking to save a park, building, church, or even a water fountain. Which Norman had saved as well when he produced a photograph of a young Marilyn Munroe taking a sip of water on a hot summer day. The photograph was never authenticated, and the image was hazy. But since there was enough doubt about the photograph no one had the energy to challenge Norman and ultimately the water fountain was saved.

Today, Norman was putting his talents and passions to work to save The Hotel Pennsylvania from either complete demolition or conversion into what he sourly referred to as 'a lifeless office tower'.

Norman stood a lanky six feet and his skin paled against the blackness of his suit and dark circles clasped the base of his brown eyes exposing his lack of sleep. Norman's curly mop of hair, still wet from the rain, shook along the edges of his frayed shirt collar as he pounded a gavel on the top of the oak podium that seemed to be missing a microphone. Another cut-back, Andrew was sure. Eventually, the sound of the thunder subsided, and Norman's voice was still barely audible in the cavernous room, making it seem that he was unaccustomed to speaking to a crowd. Norman had to shout over the group that gathered in the room to project his voice without the use of a microphone. This only succeeded in making him look angry and not altruistic, which anyone who knew Norman, knew him to be.

Andrew removed his trench coat and took a seat at the end of a row next to an empty chair, about one third from the back of the room. He sat down and neatly folded his coat over his left knee and consciously avoided eye contact with anyone in the room as the meeting got underway.

"Why are we even having this meeting? Everyone knows it's time for this monstrosity to be gone!" The voice came from behind where Andrew was sitting, and without turning around he recognized the sharp twang as that belonging to Ben Single. Ben was a real estate agent and was infamous for encouraging rezoning of old buildings and then slipping in as the agent of choice when it came to filling the spaces with tenants. He was here not because he cared for the fate of the hotel. He was present because he wanted to make sure whoever won the contract for the rezoning had a chance to see he was on their side from the beginning.

"Ben, we all know your stance on what should happen with the hotel. This is an opportunity for *everyone* to have a say," Norman looked around the room hoping someone else would speak up and rescue him.

"Why is the city not considering the space for some much-needed low-income housing?" Margaret Fieldstone was always present at these meetings and even though Andrew often did not agree with her, he admired her tenacity and focus. She was instrumental in securing housing and rent breaks for poorer residents in the city and that was something Andrew found hard not to respect.

Soon the shouts and claps started to come from every direction in the room, and so quickly that Andrew had trouble following which people were shouting or clapping.

"We need a boutique hotel," shouted a man from the right side of the room.

"What we need is another museum! The museums always have the right funding and attract a lot of tourists," a woman at the front declared.

"A new arena," a deep voice boomed from behind Andrew.

"There's already one across the street, you idiot!"

"Sports! It's always sports."

"An office tower. A nice glass one too."

Norman began to bang the gavel rapidly against the wobbly oak podium once more and this time, the crowd quieted down immediately.

"Look, the purpose of this meeting, in case you forgot to read the pamphlet, is to find a way to *save* the hotel. Now, is there anyone who has anything of use to contribute to this meeting, or not? Otherwise, we may as well all go home to see if our homes are flooded yet."

Margaret crossed her arms in a huff and complete visible frustration, once again, because she was unable to share the statistics she had compiled in preparation for this meeting. Ben wasted no time and began to hand out his business card to the five building developers that were standing next to him at the back of the room. The room echoed the awkward silence. Andrew listened to the pounding of the rain and knew there was no way to avoid what he had to do today even though many people were going to be displeased with his announcement.

Andrew placed his folded coat on the empty chair beside him as he stood. The sound of the light plastic chair being pushed across the rough, worn-down carpet vibrated through the damp room. The many eyes in the room followed his every step. Coerced under the weight of familial guilt, Andrew slowly walked to the front of the room and towards where Norman stood. Those that knew Andrew wondered what he could possibly have to offer to this community engagement meeting.

Without invitation Andrew centered himself behind the podium, pushing Norman off to the side.

He scanned over the crowd in the room and inadvertently locked eyes with the developers he was trying to avoid, who were standing at the back of the room. Andrew nervously cleared his throat, and as he began to speak, he hoped this wasn't going to sink his career.

2

Clarington, June 6th, 1919

In reality, Rose was thankful for having only one small suitcase since she intended to leave any remnants of her life here - in the past. Buried in Clarington, Ohio. Rose closed her suitcase for the fifth and final time, having completely reassured herself that she hadn't left anything important behind. Not that there was much to pack anyhow. Her dresses were simple and sturdy and designed for the work she was responsible for on the farm as well as in the feed store where she worked every Wednesday and Friday since she was fourteen. Her clothing material was thick to prevent fraying and ripping, and dark in color to hide any stains that she would inevitably accumulate in the process of carrying out her chores throughout the day. They were practical, like most other things in Rose's possession.

Her mother had begun to put aside items for Rose's hope chest soon after she was born. The cedar chest was handmade by Rose's father the year after she was born. It was a simply designed box with very little ornamentation except for the initials of her name, RMF. It was sturdy and stained a honey gold color and measured three feet by two feet and was deep enough to hold everything her mother thought she would require later in life. Things that every good, reliable Ohio farm wife would want to have in her possession as she began to build her life and raise a family on the plot of land where she and her new husband would begin their life of labor. There were instruments for sewing, mending, cooking, and of course the beginnings of a collection of baby clothes intended for the large number of children that were expected to diligently follow the wedding. The honey stained hope chest sat at the end of her bed as a stern reminder of the position and path her life was chosen to take. However, this collection of items were addendums to Rose's life, not things that would ever represent Rose as a person. She was amazed how her mother was able to gather such a large quantity of items considering the lack of money they had available for food and clothes, and especially with Rose being the youngest of nine children.

All nine of them girls.

This is important to note, as having girls created additional costs that arose when it was time to find a suitable husband. Costs for house making and motherhood that were assumed to be undertaken by the girls' parents. And indirectly implied the value to be placed on the girl who was to be wed. It was obvious to Rose that ensuring each daughter was married off to a hard-working suitor was as important to her parents as bringing in a profitable crop each year.

It was, she learned, her misfortune to be born into a family of nine daughters to a mother who didn't talk about her past and a father who wouldn't acknowledge the future. It was the fate of the women in her family. There was no discussion or consideration for what Rose or any of her sisters would *want*, only what the community felt they needed and where their place was set. It wasn't that Rose disliked the idea of a life married and with children, in fact, she wanted that very much. What was difficult was the idea that the decision was made for her even before she was able to walk.

Although she was the youngest and born smaller than any of her sisters, Rose Margaret Farnsworth stood just a bit shorter than her father's six feet, and taller than her sisters at five-ten. She had the same chestnut brown hair and eyes as her mother and a soft complexion that remained slightly darker than her sisters' skin through the winter. Her mother would say that it was because she was full of sunshine. Her father said it was because she was the only one of his daughters that wasn't averse to hard work. Frank and Dorothy Farnsworth were both loving and caring parents but were often preoccupied with making sure their daughters would be 'taken care of' as they entered their adult lives. Something Rose didn't think too much about. Rose was naturally strong and athletic with a permanent rose to her cheeks and was a bit more of a tomboy than her mother would have liked, but that her father was thankful for. The softness in her eyes and smile countered the intimidation that was unfortunately common for girls of Rose's height and because of that she made friends easily.

Rose had been one of the lucky girls in the small farming town of Clarington, Ohio. She had fallen in love with Robert James Wilson when she was only five years old and he was a much more mature nine. Clarington was a small town and held the regrettable distinction of having a young population base that was eighty percent female, which made dating competitive, and friendships among parents of the eligible young girls somewhat tense. Rose followed Robert everywhere and held on to every word he uttered. She would sketch pictures of him every evening in her book as she recalled what she saw him doing that day. Whether it was when Robert was climbing trees with his friends or carrying bags for the overly attentive mothers as they shopped for supplies in one of the three stores in town. She would capture the subtle lines that crept from the left side of his mouth when he smiled and the uneven; however, charming angle of his hairline. Rose had memorized everything about Robert from the way he walked, his favorite food (Buckeye Candy) to the sound of his voice. Rose was twelve when she realized that Robert felt the same way about her and for the last five years the two were inseparable.

Their families had happily agreed to their marriage and when the relief set in that one more daughter was soon to be in the safe care of a husband, Rose's parents began to focus their attention on their last unmarried daughter, Betty, who was ten months older than Rose.

A short time before their planned wedding date, Robert fell ill to the influenza outbreak that rapidly spread across the country. Rose never left his side and prayed daily for any sign of recovery; however, Robert soon became one of the over half million people in the country to succumb to the devastating effects of influenza. And within a few weeks, Rose was standing numb in the same church where she and Robert had planned to be wed and was reciting the burial rights praying that Robert's soul would quickly enter heaven. Amen.

Rose grew numb and instantly withdrew from her friends and any outings that would risk the chance she may run into anyone from Robert's family.

It was two weeks after the funeral that marked the first time Rose had ever yelled at her parents. As she stood in front of the fireplace, red-faced in the center of their small living room, she felt a merciless pressure build inside her. She felt as if her world was closing in around her and she had the frightening feeling as if she was being drowned when her father announced she was to be married to Ernest Russell. Rose's rapid breathing only made her tears more uncontrollable and her voice shakier as she protested with an equal mix of fear and rage. Ernest Russell was the only single male in Clarington that held the distinct honor of reaching the age of thirty-three with not one offer of marriage in a town where women outnumbered the men four to one. And whom others said was so unassuming he didn't even warrant a middle name.

"That's not fair!" shouted Betty, who believed she was the next in line to be married.

"Fair? There is no way any of this is fair!" yelled Rose at her in response.

Rose's father was growing anxious with age and worried that his daughter would end up a spinster and soon too old to be a viable wife to any young man that owned property. And although Rose did not enjoy the prospect of being alone, she disliked the notion of being Mrs. Ernest Russell even more.

It was a few days after her confrontation with her parents that Rose's mother approached her with the surprising option of moving to New York to live with her cousin in the small borough of Brooklyn. Joseph Thomas Beman was her second cousin twice removed and was from a part of her mother's family that Rose had never met or that her parents ever spoke about. Rose's mother secretly had cringed at the thought of any of her daughters marrying Ernest Russell and set to work behind her father's back to arrange an alternative escape for Rose. Sylvia Dixon, the head of the church fundraising committee, was to be that alternative. She had a niece who was a '*rising star*' (Sylvia's words) in the hotel business in New York and was looking for young girls to fill much-needed positions in a new hotel opening in the center of New York City. With a large number of deaths due to the influenza outbreak, there was surely a need and a place for Rose among the staff. Without a second thought, Rose agreed to the opportunity and set about organizing her few possessions and hurriedly packing them into what was supposed to be the suitcase she carried with her into her married life. Rose packed with eagerness, filled with the excitement of the adventure that lay before her. She tried; however, to not display too much enthusiasm when her father was looking on, aiming to protect his feelings. He was not completely comfortable with sending Rose to New York City; however, her mother convinced him that she needed time away after Robert's death if she were to make a suitable wife to another young man. There was no return trip or date discussed and although Rose's father presumed she would return, Rose had a distinct feeling that she wouldn't be coming back.

Rose decided to leave behind all her clothes except for the few dresses she sewed in preparation for her new life as Robert's wife. Dresses that she admired from the pages of the Vogue magazine that was brought in especially for Mrs. Twindle and kept hidden behind the counter at the feed store until she would come in on Fridays. Rose would take the opportunity to glance at the pages, and she would often lose herself in the fashion and glamour of the lives that seemed so far away from Rose's life in Ohio. With her intricate artistic ability, Rose would sketch the dresses she dreamed about in her private sketch pad and along with notes about her favorite movie stars. She would keep them safely tucked under her mattress for the day she could afford a dress like the ones in the magazine or travel to the glamourous cities written about. Like Paris, London, and New York.

Rose's father would not have approved of the frivolous spending of 'hard-earned' money on the magazine so Rose would arrive early every Wednesday when the deliveries would arrive and would sneak away to the back room and carefully flip through the pages before she would wrap it up again in fresh brown paper, just as Mrs. Twindle had requested. It appeared that Mr. Twindle also felt it was a frivolous way to spend hard-earned money and the regular purchase was kept hidden from him inside the brown paper wrap and noted as 'supplies' on her receipt.

Rose enjoyed working for Mr. Burrow who had inherited the feed shop from his parents and marveled at the way he knew the intricacies of each customer and would go out of his way to make shopping easy for each of them, especially the women who Mr. Burrow had a soft spot for. Mr. Burrow also had a warm spot in his heart for Rose ever since she began to work for him at the feed store at the age of fourteen. He never forgot the summer of the drought when she offered to work for free when Mr. Burrow had worried, because of waning sales, that he would not be able to pay Rose her full salary.

"You'll get me back," Rose had said when Mr. Burrow had initially protested and then insisted on writing out a repayment plan so that Rose could keep track of her hours in the shop. Rose never collected the extra pay and refused every time Mr. Burrow brought the subject up in conversation.

About five months before her wedding, Mr. Burrow had presented Rose with a package of material, ribbons, and thread he had specially ordered from Chicago.

"I have been watching you admire the dresses in the Vogue magazine that comes for Mrs. Twindle every month and, although I cannot afford to buy you any of the dresses, I think with your talented sketches and ability to sew you should be able to make some lovely dresses for your new life with Robert," Mr. Burrow handed the large package to Rose with shaking hands and a tear in his eyes. The material was carefully wrapped in brown paper and delicately held together with a soft pink bow. "You deserve something nice to wear."

That evening Rose ran all the way home and took the whole week to carefully plan out the patterns. When she was done, she had completed five dresses and even had enough left over to make a shirt that Robert could wear on their wedding day. Instead, she had buried him in that same fine shirt she finished earlier that month.

Rose packed four of the dresses not sure if they would be appropriate for New York City but positive they would be better than the dresses she usually wore. She left out the periwinkle blue dress with a small white-flowered pattern, pearled button, and laced neck to wear on the train to New York. Along with her knitted white sweater and matching white gloves.

When Rose was ready to leave, she gave each of her sisters a hug goodbye and insisted that only their mother and father take her to the train station since it was such a long way from home. Rose faded in and out of the conversation on the way to the station. Her excitement made it difficult to focus on what she and her parents spoke about, but she did recall her father's conversation was peppered with warnings of strangers, and her mother made her promise to remember everything she saw and to write often. Both pieces of advice that Rose intended on keeping.

They arrived twenty minutes before the train was scheduled to depart and she found it waiting in the station when they arrived. The smoke rose from the stack like a beacon to Rose and she was immediately drawn towards it. The platform was filled with eager passengers saying goodbye to loved ones and porters that busied themselves with lugging cases and travel chests onto the train and into the appropriate travel cars. When Rose handed her sole suitcase to the flushed porter he nodded and smiled with relief at the lightness of the case and hurried it to her cabin where he instructed it would be waiting for her on her bed.

After a tear-filled farewell, Rose did not hesitate as she turned and marched towards the awaiting train. She stepped gingerly onto the metal step and with a slight bounce, lifted herself over the next two steps into the car and walked past the same porter whom she handed her bag to earlier. Rose made her way to cabin 1412 and rushed to take the seat by the window and watched as a combination of smiles and tears waved off the passengers as the train began to pull out of the station. As the train lurched towards New York and away from Clarington, Rose pulled her knit sweater closed and settled back in her seat to prepare for the journey. Knowing she would never call Clarington home again.

3

The screeching on the metal rails pierced the ears of the child sitting across from Rose and caused him to cry and grab the side of his head, but to Rose, the sound was music to her ears. It alerted Rose of their approach into New York City. As the train began to slow to its stop, it ricocheted off the curves of the rail as they approached Grand Central Terminal. Rose held her head out of the window and marveled at the enormity of the train station and the sounds from the surrounding platforms which grew louder as the train approached the terminal. She was feeling more like a child than the one seated across from her. Even though Rose read about what to expect, nothing could have prepared her for the actual feeling she experienced as she watched the train move towards such an incredible structure. She could hardly believe it would fit inside! As the train began to brake, Rose grabbed hold of her case and excitedly made her way towards the exit and waited for the train to come to a complete stop, and for the door to be opened and the steps to be lowered. She wanted to be the first passenger to disembark from the train car and step onto the platform below.

Rose had memorized the photograph that her mother gave her of her cousin Joseph and scanned the crowd for his face, which she soon realized would prove difficult with the mass of travelers that crammed around her. When she couldn't find him, she decided to follow the crowd of passengers as they walked towards the inner sanctum of the terminal. Rose took ten steps and then fell to a complete stop. Passengers pushed past her on both sides as she stood transfixed on the enormous columns, ornate with carvings, and had to stand still to take it all in. She glanced up towards the ceiling where she felt as if she had been transported to the top of a mountain as she scanned the collection of stars that depicted astrology signs. She remembered reading in one of the magazines that came for Mrs. Twindle about how fates were written in the stars according to the month you were born in but was completely unprepared for the astounding beauty of the ceiling. Rose turned her body around slowly moving her feet in a counterclockwise direction. With her head tilted back, and her hand tightly clutching the ivory white handle on her small case, she hunted to find the astrological sign that represented the month she was born in. No sooner had she found it; her eyes diverted to the star sign next to hers which was Robert's.

Rose whispered to herself, "You would have loved this Robert." And in some odd way, she believed he would be glad she was in New York.

She lowered her head and continued to walk in the direction that the other passengers were headed and suddenly noticed the large number of lights that adorned the inside of the station. If she had to guess, Rose was sure that the whole of Clarington didn't have as many light bulbs as there were inside Grand Central Terminal. Decorative sconces hung on the walls and posts inside the station and illuminated the enormous interior space where thousands of passengers traveled daily. At the same time, light streamed in from the arched windows that lined the highest part of the inside of the station. Beams swollen with warmth from the sun, danced across the floor as they were broken with the moving feet of the hurried passengers as they made their way towards their destinations. She continued to walk towards the exit following the hordes of passengers that had disembarked from the train, but unlike Rose, they seemed to know where they were going. Rose could feel the heels of her new shoes as they struck the marble floor a little differently than on the gravel path leaving their house and knew even though she was in the center of a train station she was in more elegant surroundings than she had ever been in. She believed that in an instant the train station could be transformed into a dance hall. And she was sure that if she were not surrounded by thousands of passengers the sound of her heels, as she walked across the floor, would send a reverberating tapping sound through the terminal and around the coved domed ceiling.

It was spectacular.

"Rose! Rose! Rose!" a repeated cheerful shout of her name sent her head spinning from side to side as she scanned the faces in the waiting crowd. As her eyes rolled over the top of the crowd, she noticed an arm waving in her direction and when she took a closer look, she could see it was the same man from the picture. It was her cousin Joseph, and Rose breathed a deep sigh of relief.

Joseph Thomas Beman was much taller than she thought he would be, but his distinctively good looks and broad shoulders were easy to recognize. The picture that Rose committed to memory was taken during a Christmas gathering several years earlier. He was seated on a yellow floral couch, squeezed in between his two younger twin brothers; where the photographer seemed to catch the three amid a joke revealing Joseph's distinctive smile. Joseph looked much younger in the photograph and his naturally curly hair was left to its own devices at the time. Now, Joseph wore his charcoal black hair smoothed down with some sort of salve and brushed back into place where he held it down with a light brown newsboy style cap.

Rose smiled and waved in return as she moved towards where Joseph stood waiting. As she grew closer to him, she noticed his light wool suit was a shade darker than the newsboy cap that was perched on the top of his head. The bright white shirt looked freshly starched and the dark black-tie held tightly to his athletic frame, emphasizing his strong physique. Rose was within a few steps from where Joseph was waiting and wasn't sure if she should greet him with a handshake or a hug since he was family. Luckily Joseph alleviated her decision by reaching for her suitcase with his left hand and simultaneously extending his right.

"Am I ever glad I found you so quickly, Joseph!" Rose exclaimed, "I was not ready for such a large crowd."

"It's Joe," her cousin corrected her with a smile, "and you better get used to the crowds. There are over five million people living here."

The look of shock on Rose's face drew a deep laugh from Joe that was reminiscent of the photo she had used to identify him earlier.

Joe walked beside Rose and while carrying her suitcase in his left hand, he placed his right on her back and guided her through the crowd, towards the exit, and then they turned left as they walked through the doors that spilled onto the street. The noise inside the station was no match for the sounds that greeted Rose on the street. There was so much noise that Rose initially couldn't recognize where they were all coming from.

It was late afternoon and people were hurrying with definite purpose towards their next destination. Some were most likely heading home; however, Rose had heard that there was a lot to do in the city and that many people would stay behind to socialize after work before returning home. Rose wouldn't know where she would have veered off to in Clarington when she left work on Friday's after working in the feed shop. Outside of sitting with her sketchbook next to Nettly Creek which wound its way through town, there was nowhere else to go.

"Is it always so busy here?" Rose leaned close to ask Joe as they walked towards an even busier street directly ahead of them.

Joe nodded to the next block, "That's 7th Avenue and yes, it's always this busy. You are going to need to get used to it since you are going to be around this area a lot," Joe pointed to the left when they reached the corner of 42nd Street and 7th Avenue, "the hotel is that way about ten blocks."

Rose strained to look around the people walking in front of her and glanced down the street. It was longer than any street she had ever seen before and each side was flanked with rows of tall buildings. Each one was decorated with carved stone, emblems, statues, or brick patterns. Rose's eyes naturally crawled upwards with the uncontrollable draw of the buildings' height and her senses fought between the onslaught of sights and sounds that filled the street.

Joe tapped her shoulder, "I am going to take you by the hotel, so you at least know what it looks like when you arrive your first day tomorrow."

Rose already knew what the hotel looked like since Mrs. Dixon had given her a postcard of the hotel that she received from her niece when it opened in January. However, Rose was happy for the preview and a chance to memorize the layout of the streets surrounding the place she would soon be spending many hours each day.

Joe guided Rose across the street and pulled her as he quickened his pace towards a waiting trolley, "You are going to want to grab the rail inside the door as you hop up on the step," Joe instructed Rose as he stood behind her. Rose knew that Joe was being extra cautious and in any other circumstances Rose would have been offended at the assumption that she wouldn't be able to hop up on the trolley without directions. However, until she felt completely comfortable with her surroundings, she welcomed any advice.

Not long after they boarded the trolley it heaved forward causing each passenger to sway slightly towards the rear of the trolley before they straightened up again and began their smooth journey south. Rose peered out the trolley's dusty window and felt a rush of excitement along with the warm Spring breeze as they passed each block along 7th Avenue, each one seemingly busier than the next. She could feel the anticipation build as they neared the hotel. Her heart was beating with so much excitement that she could feel her veins pulse along the sides of her neck.

"We get off at the next stop," Joe leaned in next to Rose's ear and nodded with his head towards the street where a crowd of passengers was waiting to board the trolley when it stopped.

Like an expert New Yorker, Rose bounced off the trolley and stepped gingerly onto the sidewalk knowing that Joe was only a few steps behind.

"How are the crowds? Overwhelming?" Joe asked with a grin.

"I love it!" Rose beamed.

Joe laughed, "You are braver than I was. I remember the first time I came down here and I thought I would never figure out this city. I got lost a few times, but now it's home." Joe pointed across the street, "There she is. The Hotel Pennsylvania."

Rose glanced across at the 22-storey building that spanned a whole city block. Sections of the hotel soared from the main floor lobby in perfectly angled columns, inviting light into the many interior rooms through the oversized windows. The windows gleamed and reflected the slowly setting sun in the west. Each window was adorned with drapes that hung inside the rooms, and not one was pulled closed. The sidewalk in front of the hotel was alive with movement. Guests were arriving with mounds of luggage that was being attended to by neatly uniformed staff who hurried to remove the bags from cars and cabs and swiftly carried them into the hotel lobby. Guests were greeted by smiling doormen that tipped their hats with one hand while holding open the large glass and brass doors with the other. As some guests were arriving, others were exiting and walking north along 7th Avenue most likely towards shopping or a restaurant. The thought of dinner made Rose's stomach grumble, but she placed her hand on her stomach and forced the feeling away, not wanting to be distracted from the buzzing excitement taking place around her.

"I can't believe how many people there are here. I read in The Saturday Evening Post that New York is busy all day long, but I never imagined how it would feel," Rose gushed.

Joe nodded, "I didn't know how much you would know about New York. Look, any questions, just ask. I'm here to look out for you," Joe placed his right hand on Rose's shoulder and motioned with his head towards the resting hand on her stomach, "And part of that is going to make sure you get fed tonight."

Rose followed Joe as they walked down West 33rd Street until they reached Andrew's Diner situated halfway between 7th Avenue and 8th Avenue. Rose could smell the aroma that enticed the evening dinner rush as they neared the restaurant. Rose was introduced to another facet of New York City life the moment Joe pulled open the door to the restaurant. The happy chatter and clanking of cutlery breed excitement in its patrons. Rose could instantly sense that mealtime in New York City was as much about the social activities as it was about food.

The savory scent of grilled onions and rosemary blended with the distinct aroma of roast beef that had been slow-cooked for hours overtook them as they entered the restaurant. Fried potatoes carried a hint of an herb or spice that Rose had never smelled before but awoken her sense of hunger.

"I hope you're hungry, this place is to die for," Joe, still in possession of Rose's suitcase, followed the hostess as she led them to a booth at the rear of the diner and was situated next to the window.

Joe slid Rose's suitcase across the red vinyl bench seat and slipped off his cap and sat perched more on the edge than the middle of the bench. Rose took the seat across from him and although she could have managed to carry her suitcase, she was relieved to have Joe carry it for the remainder of the evening.

The hostess handed Rose and Joe the menus and after a little deliberation Joe ordered the special, roasted beef and garlic potatoes, and Rose followed suit. She wondered if it was the scent of garlic that intrigued her. Her mother never strayed from the five recipes that her father liked, two being salt and pepper, and as a result her culinary tastes never developed beyond those few flavors. And with Clarington's lack of restaurants, there was no opportunity to explore any cultural or culinary variances.

Their meals arrived a short time later and Rose devoured her meal as quickly as Joe did and would be sure her mother would have admonished her if she had seen how quickly Rose cleared her plate. Dorothy Farnsworth would say, 'a lady rarely finishes her whole meal and never before a man' and in response to which Rose would roll her eyes and her sisters would laugh.

After they were finished Joe ordered two pieces of New York apple pie and he insisted Rose try a slice, "I wouldn't turn it down if I were you," Joe warned, "my kitchen isn't exactly well-stocked at the moment. And I am working tonight so I won't be around if you need anything."

Rose realized she had no idea what Joe did for a living. She was just so excited to have moved to New York that she didn't think about the side details like her cousin's job. "Where do you work Joe?"

Joe scooped a spoonful of the warm cinnamon apple pie into his mouth and nodded his head from side to side as chewed then swallowed the piece. "This and that."

When Rose's looked confused by his answer he added, "I provide supplies to local Jazz clubs in the city and since they operate in the evening," Joe took a sip of his coffee, "so do I."

Jazz clubs, Rose thought, sounded terribly exciting and exactly where her parents would not want her to be during her time off work.

Joe swallowed a mouthful of pie, "You ever been to a Jazz club?"

"No," Rose shyly replied.

Joe waved the fork he held in his hand wildly in the air, "You'll love it." An assumption more than an offer, Rose thought.

After their meal, Joe walked Rose back to the station where they rode the subway from downtown New York City to his apartment in Brooklyn. Rose was beginning to tire and after Joe showed Rose her room and where to find the necessities in his small apartment, he left for work.

"I will be here when you wake up and show you the way to the hotel in the morning," Joe promised as he hurried out the door for the evening.

When the door closed behind Joe, Rose turned and looked around at the small dusty apartment, that Rose learned was lucky to have two good sized bedrooms and a private bathroom, unlike most apartments in the area. Joe hadn't exaggerated when he said he did not have a well-stocked kitchen. Rose opened the cupboards and except for a few cans of soup, some coffee, tea, and a bowl of discolored hardened sugar, there was nothing to eat. Rose opened his small icebox that stood in the corner of the room and a half jug of milk and another with pungent clear liquid and a hardened block of butter stood bare under the small stream of light that eked in from the side window.

Rose vowed to pay Joe back with some real homecooked meals once she figured out where to buy some food. Rose looked around the room that was now her home and where she would be spending her time while off work. The small windows were streaked with dust and grime and when Rose dragged her finger over the glass, she realized both sides of the windows needed a vigorous cleaning. The floors showed streaks from dirty shoes and spilled drinks that were poorly wiped and then collected further patterns of dirt outlining the spill like a crime scene. A foul-smelling damp towel was draped over the back of one of the kitchen chairs and the tables and shelves were devoid of pictures or any ornamentation. This unquestionably was the bleakest home, or version of a home, that Rose could ever have imagined living in.

And she instantly loved it.

Absolutely and completely loved it. Rose pulled off her sweater and after finding a couple of rags and some soap she set about to clean Joe's apartment for the next couple of hours. When she was done the same small, bleak, dirty apartment had been transformed into a small, bleak, clean apartment. Then completely overwhelmed with exhaustion, Rose went about setting her things up in her room, hanging her few dresses in the closet and tucking other personal items of clothing and toiletries in the three-drawer dresser Joe had cleaned out for her use.

Rose set her hair after a quick bath and slipped into bed after she made sure the door and windows were locked. Something she never thought about in Clarington, but instinctively did now.

As she watched the night darken through her window, the events of the day cycled through Rose's mind as she replayed each moment of her first day in New York, until exhaustion finally dragged her mind into a deep sleep.

4

As she looked out of the dust-covered windows into the steely grey morning sky Rose knew the day was going to be perfect. The smell of coffee pulled Rose from her slumber and once she opened her eyes, she realized that she hadn't thought about what she would eat for breakfast before she left for work. In fact, she hadn't thought about what she would do for the rest of the day for food. No matter, she thought. Rose didn't hesitate as she bounded out of bed and hurried to dress for work. She unwound her hair and did her best in the poorly lit room to style her hair for the day. Since her selection of dresses was small, it didn't take Rose long to choose the green dress from the closet. She remembered back to when she unwrapped the gifted package of cloth from Mr. Burrow and saw the white polka-dotted green material. She immediately knew she would make a dress she would come alive in. She had planned to wear it on her first official day as Mrs. Robert Wilson and felt her first day of working at The Hotel Pennsylvania was the most fitting replacement.

Rose slipped on her shoes and once she was pleased with her appearance, she left her room and joined Joe in the kitchen.

"Morning," Rose bounced into the room just as Joe was setting food on the kitchen table along with the freshly brewed coffee.

"Morning! How'd you sleep?" Joe asked as he busied himself with the lid of the jam jar. "I didn't expect you to do all that cleaning last night, although, I can't say I wasn't pleased. Thanks."

"You're welcome," Rose replied, "But I know none of this food was here last night." Rose sat down at the table and inhaled the robust aroma of the dark coffee as it wafted up around her along with the sweet scent of the toasted buns Joe had arranged on a plate in the center of the table. "These are bagels, right?"

Joe nodded and smiled, "Yeah, do you have these back home?"

Rose shook her head, "No. I read about them in one of the magazines that came for Mrs. Twindle at the shop I worked at. I always wanted to try one."

Rose reached out and grabbed a warm bagel and took a bite. The sweetness of the bread along with the melted butter enveloped her mouth and made her realize she was hungrier than she usually was in the morning. The coffee Joe brewed was richer than the coffee her mother brewed at home. Rose figured it was either due to different beans he was able to buy in New York or because he didn't have to resort to rationing the grinds. With eleven mouths to feed, Rose's mother often thinned out soups and stews and would leave out the full required measurements of sugar and spices when cooking. Coffee was no exception.

"This is great Joe," Rose thanked him as she gulped the rest of her coffee feeling satiated and energetic from the surprise morning meal.

"I grabbed some food from the club last night as well as some food for you to have at lunch today," Joe pointed to a bag on the counter that was wrapped and ready for Rose to take. "I wasn't sure what you liked to eat so I just had the cook put together a sandwich and some cookies for you."

Rose wiped the corner of her mouth with the napkin Joe set on the table. She noticed the initials GE embroidered on the corner in a fine black thread but didn't mention it. "I can't believe I start today. I am so excited. I just hope I don't embarrass myself," Rose confessed to her worry.

"Nah, you'll be fine," Joe pushed his chair back and began to clear the table, "We should head out soon so I can get you to work a little bit earlier. It's always good to show up looking eager on your first day. It's the first day that everyone remembers."

As they walked towards the train, Rose was thankful for Joe's company on her first day at work. They boarded the subway five blocks from Joe's apartment and Rose memorized the surroundings to make sure she would remember exactly in which direction to go. She had a knack for remembering things easily which gave her an advantage in school; however, she never had to memorize her way around town since Clarington was too small to get lost in.

Rose was happy to learn that it was one train she had to ride into work. She also knew that she would have no trouble remembering where to disembark as well since the station held the same name as the hotel.

Rose slid through the entrance gate, keeping close to Joe and making sure she didn't get lost in the morning crowd. The platform was filled with people mostly smiling and chatting as they made their way into the city. Some people; however, displayed a look of exhaustion revealing that they were either up late the night before or did not enjoy the busy life that New York had to offer. Rose felt a sudden rush of warm air as the subway approached the inside of the station and in an instant, it swirled around her twisting the bottom of her dress around her legs and she quickly shifted her arms to stop it from rising. Expert passengers turned their bodies to face the approaching car and jostled into position preparing for the doors to slide open. Unsure of the safest place to stand, Rose positioned herself directly beside Joe close enough that their elbows touched.

Joe, sensing her fear wrapped his left arm around her back, "Don't worry, just follow me there is nothing to be afraid of."

Rose shot Joe a grateful smile and nodded.

When they reached Penn Station, Rose and Joe exited onto the platform and, along with several other passengers exited to 33rd Street above. Joe walked Rose to the corner of 7th Avenue and stopped. "Okay, you got this from here Rose. Just go in and act sure of yourself, even if you're not. There'll be time for upset later but remember make a good first impression." Joe patted Rose on her shoulder and watched her as she turned and walked towards the entrance of the hotel.

Rose's heart was pounding so loudly she was sure the people next to her on the street could hear it. As she approached the front door, she was uncertain of the etiquette she should follow, and just as she was about to ask the doorman he nodded, smiled, and stepped sideways as he held the door open for her. She clutched her purse which held a small change purse and the lunch that Joe brought for her from the club and walked inside.

It took less than a few steps into the hotel for Rose to realize the allure and excitement that The Hotel Pennsylvania possessed. Staff, in their starched uniforms emblazoned with the hotel logo embroidered on the pocket, were proudly busying themselves with guests in the lobby. Rose wondered with anticipation if her uniform would look as impressive as the ones worn by the employees in the lobby. Rose followed a young couple that entered the lobby ahead of her as they walked up the five polished steps that were enclosed with brass rails and led to an even more impressive marbled lobby. Columns of granite surrounded the grand lobby and stretched over a hundred feet towards the top of the domed ceiling. Rose slowed her walk admiring the richly painted walls that were embellished with oversized paintings and bordered with carved swirled frames that were ornately trimmed with stripes of gold. Polished mahogany tables glimmered under the many electric light fixtures that lined the halls of the hotel entrance, illuminating the interior even further and the faint scent of lemon polish was unmistakable as she walked through the hall towards the lobby. Oversized hand-painted vases sat perched in the center of each table crammed with fresh flowers and professionally styled to look as if they were naturally falling from the center of the vase. The subtle scent of the flowers trailed behind Rose as she passed by the tables on her way into the main lobby area. The lobby was lined with embroidered sofas and fashionable chairs each with an inviting arrangement that encouraged lounging and conversation and was filled with the morning musings of guests and staff as they went about their day. Some arranging meals, others looking for exciting things to do as they visited the city.

Rose turned her attention from the ornateness of the building and its interiors to the guests that filled the lobby area. Rose felt as if she was reading one of Mrs. Twindle's magazines in the back of Mr. Burrow's storeroom. Dresses, like the ones she admired from the fashion pages of Vogue or even Life Magazine, were draped around many of the women and girls as they casually made their way through the lobby. Sharply dressed men held their wives' arms and mirrored the successful businessmen profiled in The Saturday Evening Post. Rose's attention was captured by three young girls who looked to be about her age as they sat on a green lobby sofa and giggled as a handsome young man passed their way, nodded, and tipped his hat before continuing towards the enormous bank of elevators at the far end of the lobby.

Rose beamed with excitement at the scene that played out in front of her as it would have in one of her favorite silent movies. Rose imagined the lives and the conversations that must have played out daily in the lobby of the hotel. She captured the moments in her mind so when she returned home to her sketchbook, she could record them forever.

"May I help you, ma'am?" a deep voice caught Rose off guard, and she jumped as she was startled out of her daydream.

"Oh, yes. Thank you," Rose turned to face a young uniformed man who stood with his arms folded neatly behind his back and the hotel embroidered box hat atop his head. His dark blue uniform looked to be tailored perfectly to his body and the edges of the seam pressed knife sharp. Even the shine of his shoes seemed to be freshly applied. The brass tag pinned to the chest of his uniform told her his name was Sam.

"I am looking for Mrs. Miller. Mrs. Susanne Miller. I am to start work today." Rose proudly announced.

The young man's smile momentarily flattened on his face before returning to the same grin he initially greeted Rose with. "Yes, just follow me ma'am" The young man turned on his polished heels and began to walk to the other side of the lobby where he turned left and continued down a long hallway and pushed open a door that was adorned with a brass label that indicated it was the staff's entrance.

"You can call me Rose," Rose whispered behind the young man who guided her through the labyrinth beyond the lobby. She wasn't opposed to being called Miss Farnsworth but was enormously opposed to being called ma'am. Especially by someone her age.

"Pardon ma'am?" The young man asked.

"My name. It's Rose Farnsworth," Rose explained with a smile, "You can call me Rose."

"Yes ma'am," the young attendee turned and continued down the interior hallway that was painted less ornamentally than the lobby but still impeccably coated with a brilliant white coat of paint.

Rose smiled and continued to follow him down the hall until they reached the offices that the managers and supervisors occupied.

"Here you go ma'am," the young man stood sideways next to the door and instead of opening the door, he extended his left arm pointing towards the handle, keeping his right arm folded behind his back. "Mrs. Miller is just right through there."

"Thank you," Rose said as she reached for the brass handle.

The young man nodded and quickly began to return down the hall from which they just walked, "Good luck." Rose could hear him murmur as he quickened his steps away from the office.

Rose shook off her nervousness and gripped the brass handle. She breathed a deep gulp of air before turning the handle the full rotation and pushing the heavy glass and wood door open. She stepped into a bright, but small, waiting room that led to three other offices, each with a brass nameplate of the occupant of the room. Light emanated from the room to the far right. The main waiting room was lit with three wall lights and a large ceiling fixture that illuminated the brightly painted white walls. The carpet was industrial-grade but carried a fine gold swirl through the dark brown background giving it a more elegant feel.

"May I help you?" a young girl who looked to be slightly older than Rose's seventeen years, entered the room with her arms wrapped around a stack of paper. She wore her golden blonde hair twisted up and fashionably pinned in various angles on the side of her head that boldly revealed her slim elegant neck and bright green drop earrings. Her soft blue dress with a fashionable low waist accentuated her slim figure and height. She walked in shoes slightly higher than the one's Rose wore. They were white with a slim buckle that stretched up from the toes and wrapped around her equally slim ankles. Rose thought she looked more like a guest instead of a hotel employee.

"Yes, I am here to see Mrs. Susanne Miller. I am to start work today," Rose smiled a warm smile wanting to make a good first impression.

The young lady dropped the paper on the desk, placed both hands on top of the pile, and leaned over her desk to speak to Rose in a hushed tone. "First of all, it's Ms. Miller. Never Mrs. and absolutely never Susanne." She then relaxed and straightened her body and held out her right hand with a smile, "I am Helen Brown. Welcome to The Penn!"

"The Penn?" Rose reached out and eagerly accepted Helen's welcoming hand.

"Uh-huh," Helen laughed, "and yes, it's as glamourous as it seems."

"I couldn't believe it when I walked into the lobby today," Rose confessed.

Helen's face dropped, "Oh, and another thing, there is an entrance for staff. It's off 32nd Avenue, about half a block in from 7th. That's where you'll want to come in tomorrow."

Rose smiled, "There's a lot to learn."

"Where are you from?" Helen stood straight and crossed her arms, "The look on your face screams that you're not from New York."

45

"Is it that obvious?" Rose laughed.

"To someone who had that same look a few months ago, yes."

"I am from Ohio, a small town called Clarington. You probably never heard of it." Rose said.

"You're right. I haven't," Helen chuckled, "I am from Chicago. Not a small town but it was starting to feel that way, so when I saw an opportunity to work in New York I jumped at it. Where are you staying?"

"With a cousin of mine in Brooklyn," Rose wanted to explain how she managed to ride the subway for the first time today but decided it wouldn't be as exciting a topic as she thought it was. "You?"

"I am the lucky recipient of a room at Holy Rosary Parish," Helen waved off her explanation, "It was the only way my mother would let me come to New York. I had to agree to stay where Father Donovan could keep a close eye on me." And then Helen winked with a laugh.

Helen walked from behind her desk and began to lead Rose towards Ms. Miller's office, "Just don't let her intimidate you, but don't talk too much either. She is either going to like you or not like you, and there is not going to be anything you can do about it either way." Helen softly knocked two times on the door before turning the handle and pushing it open, then she mouthed the words, "Good luck," as Rose walked inside.

Rose stepped into the room clutching her purse hoping all the tension she felt would leave her face and voice and transfer to her fists. She stood quietly as she watched Ms. Miller organize a stack of papers on her desk.

After a couple of seconds, and without lifting her head, Ms. Miller spoke, "Well, what is it? I haven't all day."

"I am here to report for my first day at The Penn, Ms. Miller," Rose announced with forced confidence.

Ms. Miller lowered her pen and slowly raised her head and stabbed a glare over the top of her glasses, "It is The Hotel *Pennsylvania*." She corrected Rose, emphasizing the word Pennsylvania as she lingered over the last syllable. She then leaned back in her chair, removed her glasses, and crossed her arms, "What is your name?"

Rose fought to hold on to some shred of control but felt it slowly slip away under the scrutinizing gaze of Ms. Miller, "Rose Farnsworth, ma'am."

Ms. Miller returned her gaze to the papers in front of her and dropped her thin craggy finger and moved it down the page passing over a list of names typed along the left-hand side.

"Ah, yes. Aunt Sylvia's project," Ms. Miller surveyed Rose from her perch behind her desk. Her dark eyes rolled over Rose judging whether she would be acceptable enough to work at the hotel. Her joyless lips pursed tightly together ensuring a smile would not accidentally slip out and reveal any level of pleasantness. "I will put you in the laundry room for now until we see what you can do."

"I thought I was to be a chambermaid ma'am?" Rose immediately regretted the words as they left her lips.

"Being a chambermaid requires professionalism, refinement, and intelligence. None of which I am sure you have Miss. Farnsworth," Ms. Miller stood from behind her desk and walked directly towards the door without turning her head towards Rose and snapped, "Follow me."

Rose walked in step with Ms. Miller but not close enough to possibly offend her. Rose could feel her cheeks as they flushed and was thankful for the supportive nod and smile that Helen offered as she followed Ms. Miller out of the office and into the hallway. Ms. Miller dressed completely in line with the personality she displayed in her office. Her dark brown hair was greased in place and pulled tightly into a bun that rested on the lowest possible part of the back of her head. The dress she wore seemed to be excessively designed to not reveal any part of her body that could be mistaken as feminine. The heavy fabric reminded Rose of the canvas like fabric she fashioned her work dresses from for the feed shop, but less elegant. The plain dark brown material hung from Ms. Miller's boney shoulders and stopped about two inches below her knees. The sleeves of the dress reached the full length of her long arms and were tailored with three plain black buttons at the wrists. Dark stockings and shoes with a thick buckle completed the school matron look.

And slowly the excitement that Rose felt as she entered the office was replaced with an impending feeling of doom as she followed Ms. Miller down the hall towards the laundry room. Rose forced herself to keep her mind resolved to a positive outlook, after all, isn't that what coming to New York was all about? And with that thought, Rose stepped into the cavernous laundry room suppressing her apprehension and fear behind a feigned smile.

5

Ms. Miller stayed in the room just long enough to introduce Rose as the new 'laundry girl' to the two girls standing behind a pile of freshly washed towels and to momentarily scan their attire, but took no time to introduce the two girls to Rose. After a terse reminder that they were still under probation, and apparently disappointed to not find anything during her brief visual inspection that would require a reprimand, Ms. Miller turned on her heels and briskly left the room. As the door was closing behind Ms. Miller, the two girls looked at each other and rolled their eyes, and simultaneously shared a subdued laugh. They immediately walked over to Rose and warmly greeted her. The girls were the same age as Rose and their features were extraordinarily different from one another.

Siobhan Kelly was the first to introduce herself and Rose was to learn a true natural leader. She had immigrated from Ireland five years ago and had started working at the hotel the first day it had opened. She had moved here with her mother and two younger brothers; however, her father passed away on the ship during their trip to America. Siobhan said she had a feeling her father knew he was dying and his one last job as their provider was to see his family set up in a country with boundless opportunity. Siobhan had bright red curly hair and piercing green eyes that jumped from the contrast of her alabaster skin. She was the same height as Rose and had a slight, but athletic build. Her soft pink lips glistened with a light gloss like the ones Rose remembered reading about in the last issue of Vogue magazine. She had read that girls in Paris were wearing it as a daytime fashion trend. She was sure it was called Frosted Pink or something like that. She just remembered it being a more acceptable color for a younger girl as opposed to the deep reds worn by stars of the time. Rose briefly wondered if she should start buying makeup. Siobhan spoke rapidly and with a thick Irish accent and was quick to set Rose at ease with her smile.

Angelina Fiorino, on the other hand, was quiet in contrast to Siobhan's animated personality but equally as kind. Angelina was a few inches shorter than both Rose and Siobhan and had a thick head of black hair that was cut in a stylish bob that hung just above her jawline.

Her skin was a warm olive tone and her almond-shaped dark brown eyes had flecks of gold that shone under her long thick eyelashes. It was obvious that Angelina did not need to wear any makeup and that the slight blush in her cheeks was her natural coloring and not due to the application of rouge. Angelina had a petite frame, sincere welcoming smile and Rose was to soon learn a large family and no accent.

"Here, you are going to need to change," Siobhan waved her hand, motioning Rose to a room in the back that was lined with lockers and a bathroom. "You will find the uniforms on the shelf to the left. Once you change, put your things in one of the lockers and come out. Angelina and I will teach you the ropes."

Rose thanked Siobhan and closed the door behind her. Rose easily found a uniform in her size and changed into it quickly and placed her green dress and shoes in a locker along with her purse. In fact, Rose thought, this would make her clothes last longer until she could afford to make new ones to wear. It wasn't the uniform Rose had imagined; however, she still took a moment to admire the gold hotel emblem on the collar.

It didn't take long for Siobhan and Angelina to explain their duties in the laundry room, and just as they finished, the remainder of the staff began to arrive.

"The laundry staff generally come in a little later since most of the towels and sheets won't be down here until the chambermaids can clean the rooms. We work in shifts and since you came in at the same time as we did, you can be on our shift. At least until we hear differently." Siobhan took Rose into the area with the oversized washing machines where a couple of loads of sheets were getting ready to be washed.

The smell of the bleach and the detergent left no room for any of the glamourous scents from the lobby to filter into the room. The girls were putting on their netted caps when a cart was being wheeled in with bundles of sheets from the rooms that had already been cleaned. For the next three hours, the team in the laundry room bleached, washed, dried, and ironed sheets and towels and then folded them onto carts where chambermaids could then change them out anew for the guests. The process was simple, rote, and would otherwise have been boring if not for Siobhan's and Angelina's stories and conversation.

When it came time for their lunch break, Rose grabbed the lunch her cousin Joe put together for her and followed Siobhan and Angelina into the large staff cafeteria that was situated in the basement of the hotel.

"Next time don't bother bringing a lunch. The hotel provides food for the staff," Angelina told Rose. "At least grab a drink with us."

The three sat for half an hour and Rose realized how much she had in common with them both. Three girls from three different lives, each brought together by circumstance and chance.

"So, what brought you to New York?" Angelina asked Rose.

Rose wasn't prone to speaking about herself or her situation freely; however, things were different now for her and if she was to make any friends and a new life in New York she had to accept that.

"I was engaged to be married," Rose began.

"So young?" Angelina exclaimed.

"What are you talking about," Siobhan retorted, "You told me your mother was married at fourteen!"

"That was a different time," Angelina explained with a wave of her hand and encouraged Rose to continue.

"I come from a small town and that is just what is expected," Rose said. "There is little opportunity for school or work, and that is just what is expected of you."

"You mean women," Siobhan snapped.

Angelina rolled her eyes, "Give it a break for one day, Siobhan."

Siobhan gave Angelina a crooked smile and laughed then looked at Rose, "So what happened? If you are here, I assume you never got married."

Rose shook her head, "No, I didn't. He died from the influenza outbreak. I ended up burying him in the church I was supposed to marry him in. It wasn't fair, he really was a good guy. And in our town women out-number men four to one so when you get a good one, girls tend to hang onto them."

"Gee, I am sorry Rose," Siobhan softened her tone. "What made you come to New York?"

"Well, my parents wanted me to marry a man in town who, let's say, is lacking in desirable traits. He is often drunk, and rumors have it that he has a bit of a temper. My mom worked to find me a way out of the marriage, and the best option was to get me out of town. A lady she knows from our church is Ms. Miller's aunt, so..."

"Ah, so, she got you a job at The Hotel Pennsylvania!" Angelina finished.

Rose held out her hands, "And here I am."

"Where are you living?" Siobhan asked.

"In Brooklyn with my cousin who has been here for years," Rose explained.

Siobhan and Angelina looked at each other and smiled, "We are going to show you this city!" they cried in unison.

Rose began to grill the girls about what there is to do in New York, realizing she had found two easy friends.

"We will show you all there is to do here. It is such a great time to be a single woman in this city! There is so much more freedom. You must come with me to the women's voting group one night. Oh, and the dance clubs!" Siobhan suggested.

"My cousin works with some Jazz clubs in town!" Rose proudly announced.

"Really! Which ones? Well, we will have to get your cousin to introduce us to some late-night fun!" Siobhan hinted.

They continued to tell Rose about the late-night restaurants, parties, and shopping that gave New York the excitement and flair that was written about in magazines. Theatre was also something not to be missed and silent movie stars, stage actors, actresses, and musicians came through the hotel frequently, and if they were lucky, they could catch a glimpse or even an autograph from one.

When it was time to return to work Siobhan and Angelina took Rose through the east side of the lobby so she could get a glimpse of the splendor of the hotel mid-day.

"You can see the light shine through the top windows and it's magical," Angelina gushed.

"That's the Roman Catholic in her coming out," Siobhan let out a big laugh, but then had to agree how spectacular the lobby was in the hotel.

There was a lineup of twenty people waiting to check-in while the string of guests checking out was much shorter at only four. Rose watched from a distance as mothers and fathers hurried their children through the lobby towards the elevators, three young women were deeply absorbed in a fashion magazine; however, Rose could not make out the cover. She wondered if it was the same Vogue magazine that Mrs. Twindle was having delivered this month in Clarington. Rose could have stayed like this for hours, watching guests come and go dreaming about what they were here to do in New York and what their private stories were.

Everyone had a private story. Even in a small town like Clarington you had to keep one or two secrets to yourself.

"We should get back now," Siobhan interrupted Rose's daydream with a tap on the shoulder.

Rose turned and began to walk behind Siobhan and Angelina when she saw a girl in a green dress with white polka dots like the dress she wore to work today. It was a design she replicated from one that was featured in a Paris fashion magazine and Rose guessed that the girl in the lobby probably purchased hers in

Paris. She had almost identical features to Rose and even the same color of hair. She was walking in front of Sam, the bellhop, who was carrying an oversized trunk up to her room. The key she swung from her right hand had the room number engraved with gold print. 1783.

As Rose continued to follow Siobhan and Angelina back to the laundry room in the basement, she committed the room number to memory, promising herself that one day she would be a guest in room 1783.

6

Rose declined Siobhan's offer for dinner after work and decided to walk around the outside of the hotel while she was waiting for Joe to meet her. Rose walked most of the way with her head tilted upwards as she admired the detail and beauty of the architecture in the city. The height of the buildings was astounding, and if it weren't for her excessive enthusiasm for her new life, the grandeur of buildings and people would have threatened to overwhelm her. Before coming to New York City, the tallest building Rose had seen was three levels; however, that was the feed store and it included an attic. She walked around the hotel twice and it spanned the entire city block. She was entranced by the detail of the structure and could barely believe that buildings this size could even be built. No matter how gruff Ms. Miller was, Rose knew she was lucky to have a position at The Penn, even if it wasn't as a chambermaid as she had hoped.

As Rose walked, she turned her attention from the buildings that lifted from the ground around her, to the people that were walking on the street. Many were making their way from work, and some from home, to meet friends to either eat or to shop. Rose was sure the list of things to do was endless. She heard languages she didn't recognize and smelled scents she couldn't name. There were so many things to learn and take in while living in New York.

Her cousin had told her there were parts of the city she didn't want to walk into by herself and that every big city had rougher parts of town. Joe promised to show her the beauty of New York and to caution her about the areas she should avoid as well.

Rose stopped at a storefront window display and was mesmerized by the fashionable women's display. What grabbed Rose's attention wasn't the color or shape of the dresses, but the freedom that seemed to even exude the mannequins. There was a sense of freedom and life for young women in New York that was absent in Clarington.

As Rose took in the splendor of the window display, she caught Joe's reflection in the glass and turned to face him.

Joe ran across the street and hugged his cousin.

"How was your first day as a chambermaid?" Rose tucked her arm in Joe's elbow, and they began to walk south along 6th Avenue.

"Well, for starters, I am working in the laundry room and not as a chambermaid. Ms. Miller didn't exactly take too warmly to me. However, I met two wonderful friends that I will be working with so it's not all bad. Siobhan and Angelina." Rose said.

"Sorry about that. I know you were excited about your first day," Joe patted Rose's hand that was tucked into his elbow. "How about a nice dinner out to celebrate?"

"Oh, Joe! That is too extravagant. We can go home, and I can make us dinner there," Rose offered.

Joe held both his hands up in the air, "Do you know where you are?"

"The city that never sleeps?" Rose answered with a laugh.

"That's right! And I am going to take you to the best new Italian restaurant in town and then I am going to take you to a Jazz club." Joe announced.

"One that you work with?" Rose eagerly asked with a smile.

Joe nodded his head and smiled.

Rose had never had Italian food and didn't know what to expect. If she had known earlier, she could have asked Angelina for a suggestion of what she would start with or what she should order. Everything was so new and exciting and Rose felt like a kid on Christmas morning. She also was feeling like a child who was about to get caught doing something wrong, when the pull towards fun was too great. Everything was so unlike Clarington that Rose wondered if her parents knew what was going on if they would force her to return home. She kept that in mind and decided that she would temper her letters home with events her mother would be comfortable knowing and sharing with her father.

Joe pointed out the shops and businesses explaining what they did as they passed by them, making the forty minutes pass quickly.

They rounded the corner of Mulberry and Hester Streets and the aroma quickly overtook Rose's senses. Smells that she never knew could exist with food. How could she feel so hungry and anticipate food she couldn't recognize? The smell was nothing she could easily describe yet hung in the air so thickly that she felt she could already taste it.

The combination of scents greeted her appetite instantly and Rose had a feeling that after dining at Puglia's, eating would never be the same again.

The one smell she could distinguish from the rest was that of freshly baked bread. The buttery essence of a warm, toasty loaf as it was removed from the oven still warm from baking, was thick among the other rivaling scents.

But each one fought the other for dominance as Rose neared the restaurant. The sweet fragrance of basil resonated with her senses. She learned that food was essential to each culture and mealtime was the one uniting factor between the people of New York.

They arrived at Puglia just as the dinner rush seemed to be starting.

"Signorino e Signorina! Table for two?" a cherubic man, slightly balding, with a thin mustache in his forties greeted them with a thick Italian accent as they stepped through the doors. A small stain of sauce on his starched white shirt was the only tell-tale sign he had been near a kitchen. His crisp shirt, paired with dark pressed dress slacks, perfectly shined black shoes, and matching tie, made him look like more of a guest of The Penn than a restauranteur.

Joe requested a table by the window in celebration of Rose's first workday in New York.

They were quickly ushered to a table centered at the front window of the restaurant where a candle stood lit in the middle of a red and white checkered tablecloth surrounded by bright white plates and an assortment of cutlery.

"My name is Gennaro, please feel free to call on me should you need anything," and with a smile and a wave of his hand, he was off to greet the next couple that walked through the doors.

Rose leaned into the center of the table to whisper, "I have a confession, Joe. I have never had Italian food. I wouldn't even know what to order."

Joe smiled and waved his hand just as Gennaro had done moments ago and in a mock Italian accent he said, "With Italian food, it doesn't matter what you order, it will be perfecto!" Joe pulled his fingers to his lips and with a kiss, he sprang his fingers in the air in front of his face.

Rose let out a laugh and shook her head, "Joe, I believe you are either going to get me into trouble or show me the best of New York!"

It didn't take long for Rose and Joe to decide on what to order, and within minutes the first of many plates began to arrive. Rose was introduced to antipasto, warm crisp breadsticks fresh out of the oven, and, her favorite of the evening, Chianti.

Rose savored each mouthful as she and Joe made their way through four courses and a bottle of wine. An hour later Rose was patting the corner of her mouth with the napkin she pulled from her lap. "I think I love garlic," Rose confessed. "We have to come here again!"

"Oh, we will," Joe promised, "But there are so many restaurants in New York that I want to show you all of them." Joe pushed out his chair and dropped his napkin and a pile of bills on the table, "Let's go, the club will be hopping soon."

The name of the club was 'Billy's'. It was a relatively short walk from the restaurant, but Joe wanted to give Rose the experience of taking a cab. Joe explained to Rose that they were starting to be known more frequently as speakeasies and held the best musicians in the country. If music was the lifeblood of their generation, then speakeasies were the heart that kept it pumping. When they arrived at the club almost twenty people were congregating on the sidewalk in front of the club. Some were smoking, others leaning against the building, but everyone, Rose noticed, was relaxed and smiling. The cab came to a stop on the corner and after Joe paid the fare, he and Rose slipped out onto the sidewalk and began to walk towards the crowd of nighttime revelers that congregated in front of the club.

"Hey, Joe! I was wondering if you were going to show tonight!" A young man ran to shake Joe's hand and pat him on the back. He was younger than Joe but older than Rose and she figured him to be about twenty-four. He wore loose brown wool trousers and a white cotton shirt with the sleeves rolled up to just before his elbows. His brow glistened with sweat and a lit cigarette hung perched between two fingers on his left hand. He turned to Rose and nodded with a smile.

Joe took the cue and introduced the two, "Carl, this is my cousin Rose. Rose, this is Carl."

Carl gently shook Rose's hand and smiled, "Glad to meet you, Rose. Is this your first time at the club?"

"It's my first time in New York," Rose confessed.

Carl pushed his eyebrows up, wrinkling his forehead, "Well, you are in for a treat tonight. Billy himself is going to play while Georgina sings."

"I can't wait!" Rose followed Joe as he maneuvered his way through the crowd, shaking almost every hand along the way.

Once they were inside the club Rose could instantly feel the energy that emanated from each person inside. Three musicians sat perched on the small stage positioned at the far end of the room and they played a melodic upbeat tune that Rose had never heard before. The man on drums swung his head side to side as he brushed the skins of the drum creating a soothing yet intoxicating beat. Another man sat half perched on a stool balancing a guitar on his raised knee and fingered the strings as he strummed in tune with the drummer. On the far right of the drummer, the oldest man of the three stood swaying side to side as he played his trumpet, commanding the direction that the drummer and guitar player followed. None of them followed sheet music yet all were playing in perfect unison.

Rose could feel her upper body sway from side to side and her head was slowly nodding along with the beat.

"That's Billy up there leading them on," Joe pointed to the trumpet player who was also the owner of the Jazz club. "My table is over there," Joe pointed to the left side of the club and guided Rose as they walked over to a curved bench that wrapped around the edge of the small table facing the band.

Rose slid along the bench seat until she was sitting in the middle and Joe stayed seated on the edge as he waved towards Billy on the stage, who then nodded in response without taking a break or a breath from the beat.

A waitress came to the table with a couple of drinks and sat them on the table before leaning into Joe's ear and whispering something only he could hear. Joe nodded and smiled and slipped a few bills into the waitress's hand. "I'll talk to him after he's done."

Rose was still transfixed by the players on the stage and the music they were playing. She had never heard anything so wonderful and happy before. Rose tapped her right foot under the table and reached for the glass in front of her and raised it to her lips. By the time the smell of the drink hit Rose's nose, it was too late. The burning sensation on her tongue triggered a spray across the table.

"What is this?" Rose gasped as her eyes began to water.

Joe laughed, "It's whiskey, Rose!"

Rose attempted another small sip, then pushed the glass away and murmured, "I think I like Chianti better."

The music came to a stop and the crowd began to clap and Rose and Joe followed suit.

"Now comes the real treat," Joe said.

Rose watched as the most elegant woman she had ever seen step onto the stage and slowly centered herself in front of the musicians. Her dress was adorned with small crystal beads that reflected the light from around the room. The hem of her dress swept below the bottom of her heeled shoes and moved elegantly with each step she took. A thin necklace rested against the front of her slim neck and hung along the length of her spine, elegantly dangling as she walked. Her hair was pulled up and held in place with pearl pins with only a few strands left loose that hung fashionably along the side of her face. Her complexion was radiant and although she didn't need it, her eyes and cheeks were tinted with a small amount of makeup that accentuated her features.

This, Rose learned, was Georgina Evans.

It became apparent that the only thing that could challenge her appearance was her voice. Rose had never heard a voice that could command both strength and softness at the same time. Georgina began with a low, slow beat moving her shoulders in time with the band, and then as she crawled up the chords her body began to change, and she moved her torso in a twisting swaying motion.

Georgina continued for over an hour moving from one song to another, each one was more intoxicating than the one before. People streamed up in pairs to dance along to the music and each time Georgina strung out the final note on a song, the crowd began to clap and cheer. And then soon, Georgina would launch into another tune to which more patrons would jump up and join the crowd at the front of the club dancing.

The first three notes of the next song began two octaves higher and a few beats faster than the other songs, and soon the dance floor was flooded with exuberant people moving to each beat of the band.

"Come on Rose," Joe grabbed his cousin's wrist and pulled her out from the center of the bench, where for most of the evening she sat shielded from the draw of the dance floor.

Rose resisted, "I have never danced to Jazz before Joe!"

Joe gave Rose a friendly tug, "Don't worry."

Soon Rose was moving alongside Joe and the other members of the club on the dance floor. It didn't take Rose long to feel comfortable as she swung and twisted along to the reverberating beat and the melodic sound of Georgina's singing. The rhythm from the song pulled movement from deep within Rose enticing her body to move in ways she didn't know were possible. At one point she briefly was left feeling naked and vulnerable in the center of the club.

When the song came to an end Rose, along with the others on the dance floor, raised their arms in the air and clapped. The musicians stood and bowed, and Billy held out his right hand towards Georgina who then bowed to the crowd, who then responded with a resounding cheer.

Rose's breathing was heavy, and she could feel her cheeks grow sore from smiling. She could barely believe her first night in New York and how alive she felt.

Joe put a hand on her shoulder, "Give me a minute. I need to talk to Billy then we can go."

Rose nodded then walked to the table to retrieve her bag. She waited next to the table and watched as Joe made his way to the stage where Billy was cleaning the mouthpiece of his trumpet. The two men shook hands and were deep in conversation for about only three minutes before Billy handed him an envelope, patted him on the shoulder, and walked into the back of the room.

Joe then turned to Georgina and placed his hand on her shoulder. But not in the same manner he did with her. Rose could tell it was a more intimate touch between the two. Georgina leaned closer to Joe and whispered something in his ear, and he smiled and gently squeezed her arm.

Georgina smiled and stepped down from the stage and walked to the back of the club and disappeared into the same room where Billy went.

Joe returned to where Rose was waiting and grabbed his hat, "Okay, we can go now."

Rose stayed silent the whole ride home to Brooklyn and relived each moment of the evening in her mind several times.

After thanking Joe and excusing herself for the night, Rose found she was too excited to settle down to sleep right away. She opened the drawer to the night table next to her bed and withdrew some paper and a pen and began to write a quick letter to her mother.

She began by explaining her train trip into New York, her first day, her cousin Joe and the fabulous time she was having in the city. However, she intentionally left out the laundry room duty, Ms. Miller's sour attitude, the revolutionary speakeasy, and of course the Chianti.

Especially the Chianti.

7

In the unfashionable end of town, where New York unceremoniously steered the settlement of blacks that moved into the city, the rich culture flourished that would drive the city and the country to the forefront of music history. Segregated communities of New York City were not advertised to newcomers of the city, it was just something you learned about from locals and from living in the city. Some found out because apartments wouldn't be rented to them, others were informed by family or friends who moved to the city and found out through their own negative experience. She had learned from Siobhan and Angelina that they too were regulated to their section of town when they arrived; however, neither seemed too surprised by it.

Rose knew from the news her father and the other men in her home community talked about that segregation of people because of their color had been ended in law. It seems the minds of some of the country's citizens were trailing behind in reality. Rose remembered when she was six years old asking her mother why there weren't any black children in their town. Her mother offered a fractured smile and said she didn't know – a telltale sign that even she did not believe her own explanation.

It was some years later when Rose indulged her sense of curiosity and began to read the pages of the newsprint her father would lay on the firebox when he was done reading the news. She quickly deciphered that a community's desire to avoid the inclusion of people with different skin color had just as much to do with the color of skin but even more to do with ignorance. And it had an ugly name too. Racism. Rose was to learn the storied past of her country over the years and was saddened.

It was remnants of that type of thinking and attitude that threatened to keep Joe and Georgina apart.

Rose accompanied Joe each night as he made his rounds to three speakeasies in the city. Every time Joe timed the last stop of the night to be Billy's, and they would enter just as Georgina Evans was about to begin her set. It was easy to see that Joe and Georgina were attracted to each other. Georgina's glances to the side and an instant blush from Joe would have easily revealed to anyone watching that they were in love.

In the time he and Rose spent together Joe never once said he was in love with Georgina, but he didn't have to. It was in his eyes, and Rose thought, he surely believed that their love could go no further.

Joe tipped his hat towards the stage and guided Rose to a seat at a table against the wall. Joe ordered Rose a soda and after Billy's niece joined Rose at the table, Joe excused himself and joined Billy at the back of the club.

Joe never carried any of the gin he supplied the clubs with on these visits. Evening trips to the speakeasies and clubs allowed Joe to stay current with his customers and on the forefront of their minds, should they ever be tempted to change suppliers.

Joe had never used fear or violence with the club owners he supplied as some other suppliers did. He never had to. Instead, he was able to become part of their community by investing a deep part of himself in the success of each venture. Joe had explained to Rose that the reason he sold his gin outside of the legal channels was that his special recipe not only gave the liquid a distinct taste, it also held a higher alcohol content than was permitted by law.

The sounds of the music, the tempo of the people, and the sweet smell of the liquor-infused smoky room at Billy's became more commonplace for Rose with each day she went.

Later that evening, Rose lay in bed recounting the night. Through the thin adjoining walls of their rooms, she could hear Joe hum a tune from Georgina's set that night and prayed that the insecurity of decades of learned ignorance would lift and that Joe and Georgina could be together. Without consequence.

8

Rose plopped down onto the subway seat and strained to catch her breath. She ran the complete distance from Joe's apartment, and as she was running onto the platform the train was pulling into the station and passengers were rushing to get on. Rose clutched her purse and leaped from the platform through the doors as they began to slide closed.

She spotted a seat in the middle of the car and wiggled herself past bodies until she was able to set herself down with a thud. Her head was still pounding from when Joe burst into her room to wake her up. She had slept through her alarm and had only a few minutes to get ready for work. Joe handed a cup of black coffee and a bagel through a small slit in her door so she could eat as she was getting dressed. Rose tore a chunk of the warm, toasted bagel and popped it into her mouth, and gulped down a mouthful of the hot, black coffee as she haphazardly brushed the rollers out of her hair.

Rose hopped around the tiny room as she slipped into her stockings and tried to buckle her shoes in place, all the while trying to not spill a drop of coffee on her dress. Today she was thankful for having a uniform waiting for her at work. Rose flew out of her room ran past Joe who was holding the door of the apartment open so Rose would not have to slow down.

Rose waved as she rushed out of the apartment and down the stairwell and shouted her thanks to Joe as he wished her better luck on her second day.

Now as Rose sat in the subway, she forced herself to slow her breathing and concentrate on the day ahead. It didn't take long; however, for her mind to drift to the night before and the excitement at the Jazz club. The swaying of the subway car reminded Rose of the beat of the music and she closed her eyes as she forced the memory of the club and the sound of Georgina's voice into her mind. She silently chuckled at the memory of her spraying the whiskey across the table and the way it felt to dance along with Joe to the Jazz band. The subway car slowed, stopped, and started several times as Rose remembered the events of the night before. The car, once again, had stopped and as the whooshing sound of the closing doors sounded, Rose opened her eyes and was alarmed as she realized the train was now pulling out of Penn Station and that she had missed her stop.

Rose jumped from her seat and ran to the door and waited impatiently, tapping her foot, for the next stop to arrive, and then quickly pushed her way past the other passengers and squeezed through the doors before they were fully open. She sprang into her second mad dash of the morning and, climbing the stairs two at a time, reached the street and headed south as fast as she could run. She slowed as she approached the front doors of the hotel and then suddenly remembered the instructions to enter from the side where the staff entrance was located.

Rose turned on her heels and sprinted around the building to the side door where she dashed through the double doors and ran the length of the hallway and burst through the doors of the laundry room.

With her face flushed, and her heavy breathing making it impossible to speak, Siobhan ushered her into the back, "You better hurry up and get changed. Miller was in here already to check up on us and she will be back at any moment."

Rose stopped when they reached the changeroom door, "Oh no! I am going to get sacked!"

Siobhan twisted Rose's body around and pushed her into the change room, "Not today, I told her I sent you up to deliver some towels to a room. But hurry."

Rose quickly changed into her uniform and hurried to join Siobhan and Angelina at the folding table just as Ms. Miller walked through the door.

"Miss Farnsworth! You seem a little out of breath," Ms. Miller snapped with an accusatory tone.

"Yes, Ms. Miller. I took the stairs back down," Rose busied herself by folding the towels in front of her on the stainless-steel table. Siobhan and Angelina also did the same.

Ms. Miller stood in place for a couple of seconds longer before she turned on her heels and pushed the door open and strode out of the laundry room.

They listened as Ms. Miller's steps pounded their way back to the wing of the basement that led to her office. When they were sure she was out of earshot the three girls turned to each other and broke out into a laugh.

After a few seconds, Rose turned to Siobhan, "Thank you for covering for me."

"What happened?" Angelina asked as she lifted a large pile of folded towels onto the base of a trolley she was organizing for a chambermaid.

"I woke up late and then missed my stop," Rose explained.

Siobhan dropped her hands on the table and smiled, "There are only two reasons to wake up late and miss your stop. One, you are sick; and, two, you had too much fun last night. And seeing as you look healthy as an ox ..." Siobhan trailed off and raised her eyebrows with a sly smile waiting for Rose to answer.

Rose smiled without lifting her head.

"I knew it!" Siobhan shouted.

Angelina laughed as she busied herself at the carts.

"What did the little girl from Oklahoma ..." Siobhan began.

"Ohio," Rose interrupted and corrected.

"Ohio...do last night to make her late for work?" Siobhan finished.

"Well, after work Joe took me to an Italian restaurant called, Pu..., uh, Pug..." Rose struggled.

"Puglia," Angelina finished for her. "It is brand new. And fabulous."

Rose nodded, "Yes, very. And I had Chianti for the first time." Rose rolled her eyes back in her head to reveal the enormous pleasure she had at the restaurant.

Siobhan was growing playfully impatient, "A meal could not have possibly made you lake for work. There must be something else!"

"Well, it may have been the night out at a speakeasy," Rose teased. She thought speakeasy sounded more daring than a Jazz club.

This time Angelina's interest was piqued, and she stopped folding the towels and walked over to stand beside Rose, "What was it like?"

Both girls listened intently as Rose recounted her evening from the time Joe met her outside the hotel to the time, they left the club. Rose learned that neither girl had been to a Jazz club and that only Siobhan had tasted whiskey and Angelina knew how to make Chianti.

An alarm bell indicating a shift change shook the girls from their conversation and they hurried to finish folding the last of the towels and return them to the storage shelves.

They kept busy until their lunch break and then the three made their way down to the cafeteria to eat. Rose grabbed a tray and followed Siobhan and Angelina in line and collected a bowl of vegetable beef soup, crackers, and a drink. They sat together and ate quickly and laughed at the near-miss of the morning. When it was time to return to work the three stood from the table and began to walk back to the laundry room.

Rose stopped at the restroom door, "I will be there in a minute, I need to take a break here."

Siobhan waved as she walked on behind Angelina, "Don't be late."

Rose was only a few minutes behind them when a nervous bellhop stopped her in the hall, "You work in the laundry room, right?"

Rose nodded, "Yeah, why?"

"A guest is frantic about needing more towels and I can't find the chambermaid anywhere," the bellhop's face was flush and beads of sweat began to glisten on his brow, "If this lady complains again, I'm a goner!"

Rose, having narrowly missed the same fate this morning took pity upon the bellhop, "Don't worry. What room is she in I can run some up now?"

"Thank you. She is in room 1783." The bellhop exhaled and smiled and was gone in an instant.

Rose collected a few fresh towels and took the service elevator up to the seventeenth floor. With each ding from the elevator indicating another floor passed, it occurred to Rose that she had never been up so high in her life. Each floor brought about the excitement that made her feel more confident. When the elevator reached the seventeenth floor the brass doors slid open with a smooth motion and Rose stepped out into the lushly carpeted hall.

Each step of her foot sank into the carpet and she imagined that this is what it must be like if she were to walk on a cloud. Her steps had a slight bounce as she made her way down the hall, following the room numbers until she reached the room she was searching for.

The doors were larger than the other doors in the hotel and they had a curved panel that jutted out from the center of the door. Rose had never seen doors like this, but then again, she had never been in a hotel before either.

Rose took a deep breath and straightened her shoulders as she raised her hand and gently knocked on the door three times.

A few seconds later the door was yanked open by a young woman clad in a robe, "Yes."

"Your towels ma'am," Rose proudly announced.

The lady took the towels and shut the door without saying a word.

Rose quickly headed back to the service elevator and traveled down the seventeen floors to the lobby then made her way through the maze of halls until she reached the laundry room where she rejoined Angelina and Siobhan who was busy stuffing a large sheet into a washing machine.

The next half-hour passed silently as they bleached, ironed, and folded the sheets in preparation for the next shift.

A shock rang through the room when the door was thrown open and banged against the wall, "Miss Farnsworth!" Ms. Miller was standing at the entrance to the doorway and held a steely glare on Rose.

"Come with me," Ms. Miller smirked as she barked the order and turned and pounded her way into the hall, stopping just outside the room.

Rose walked into the hall, nervously following Ms. Miller.

"Have I done something wrong, Ms. Miller?" Rose's voice trembled as she spoke.

"Have you done something wrong?" Ms. Miller's mocking tone was unmistakable, "It depends. Did you take some towels up to room 1783 today?"

"Uh, yes I did."

"And is that in your job description?"

"No, ma'am, I just thought..."

"You are not to think, you are to *do* your job. Aunt Sylvia was wrong about you. It is only your second day and you cannot seem to follow the rules. Your job is to wash and fold towels and sheets! That's it!" Ms. Miller shoved her hands into the crutch of her elbows and held them tight across her chest.

Tears began to fill Rose's eyes and all words failed her. She wanted to apologize and beg for another chance, but the words failed to come.

"Ah, Ms. Miller, just the woman I am looking for."

Rose turned and looked towards an elegant looking man who was making his way down the hall to where she and Ms. Miller were standing. His grey suit was perfectly tailored and hemmed, and the leg of his pants just skimmed the tip of his shoe. His hair was slicked back with a type of salve or pomade that reminded Rose of how Robert would style his hair. He was a man that walked with confidence and purpose and he was making his way towards them now.

Rose looked to Ms. Miller for some indication of who this man was and was shocked to find a look of trepidation and awkwardness cross her face as this man grew closer.

"Ms. Miller, I was on my way to see you," the man looked to Rose and smiled and then turned back to speak with Ms. Miller. "I have had a remark from one of our guests about a staff member."

"Yes, Mr. Statler. How can I help."

Rose gasped; it was the owner of the hotel!

"I have become aware of one of your staff members who delivered some towels to a guest of ours, way up on the seventeenth floor," Mr. Statler motioned his finger up to the ceiling and smiled.

"Yes, sir, I am sorry about that. I am talking to the girl right now, and it won't happen again." Ms. Miller promised.

"Happen again?!" Mr. Statler exclaimed with a grin, "Why I do so hope it happens again."

He then turned to face Rose, "What is your name, miss?"

"Rose Farnsworth, sir."

"Well, Miss Farnsworth you have helped me in my attempt to impart upon our staff an important rule."

"What rule is that sir?" Rose asked.

"That the customer is always right!" Mr. Statler announced with a chuckle, "Astor thinks I am crazy, but I guarantee you it will be the way of the future for hotels. Mark my word." He then followed his statement with an exaggerated laugh and tucked his thumbs in the crutch of his suit pockets.

Rose stood transfixed on Mr. Statler who managed to suppress Ms. Miller's anger with his presence.

He turned to face Ms. Miller, "Keep up the good work Ms. Miller." He then turned to Rose and smiled.

Mr. Statler turned around and walked down the hall and made his way towards the outer corridor, whistling as he walked.

Ms. Miller, red-faced, turned her glare on Rose, "You caught a lucky break today Miss Farnsworth, but I will be watching you," Ms. Miller walked towards her office, pounding her steps as she went.

Rose covered her face with her hands and under sheer exhaustion broke down in tears.

"Hey, don't cry," a gentle voice approached her from the side.

Rose wiped her eyes, "Oh, I am sorry, I didn't know anyone was here."

The young man held his hand out offering his handkerchief for Rose, "Here, wipe your eyes. You don't want to go back to work all red-eyed."

Rose gratefully took the handkerchief and dabbed her eyes, "I don't think I am going back. I think I am done."

"Woah, that's no way for a New Yorker to talk," the stranger said.

"I am not a New Yorker. I am from Ohio," Rose explained.

The stranger laughed, "Where do you live right now?" he asked.

"In Brooklyn with my cousin," Rose smiled.

"Ah, close enough. You're a New Yorker. It doesn't matter where you're from," he held out his hand, "I am Peter. What's your name?"

"Rose," Rose returned the dampened cloth to Peter's hand and thanked him.

"Well, Rose, you need to pick yourself up and get back to work," Peter instructed.

"You heard Ms. Miller. She has it out for me."

Peter laughed, "You and every other young woman who takes a chance here. Go and prove her wrong. If Mr. Statler thought you did the right thing, you are going to be okay."

Rose smiled, "Thanks, Peter."

"You're welcome, Rose."

Rose ran the back of her hand over her eyes, removing the last of the tears from her face. She walked down the hall and began to push the door open to the laundry room then stopped and faced Peter who was watching her from where he stood in the hall.

Peter wasn't usually the type of guy Rose found attractive. He had dark black wavy hair and deep-set brown eyes and stood a little shorter than she did. Her eyes veered to the left, hoping he wouldn't catch her staring. Her cheeks quickly warmed in his presence and suddenly her vulnerability seemed exposed.

"I'll see you around," Rose's cheeks flushed red.

"I hope so," Peter winked.

She pulled just enough courage to step away from his gaze and return to the laundry room, but as she stepped out of the hall, she wanted to memorize his eyes in case she never saw him again.

9

It was the start of the third week working at The Penn and Rose had finally mastered the subway along with the workings of her alarm clock. Since her fateful second day, Rose had been able to avoid Ms. Miller completely and was starting to feel more relaxed as the days went on. She met many more people that worked at the hotel and was astounded how many people who lived and worked in New York were from somewhere else. She met people from parts of Europe she didn't know existed, tasted food she never imagined she would taste, and was continuously amazed at the vibrancy that the city had to offer.

Rose regularly sat with Siobhan and Angelina on breaks, and for the last week, Helen had started to join them as well.

"You should have seen your face when you walked into the office that first day," Helen recounted.

Rose shook her head, "I had no idea what to expect."

Siobhan teased, "And you didn't even know Peter existed!"

Her friends became aware of the attraction that Rose and Peter had for each other and they took much enjoyment at teasing Rose when the two of them would break into an awkward blush every time they passed in the hall.

"You should just ask him out," Helen suggested as she sipped her coffee.

"No! You should wait for him to ask," Angelina insisted.

"If you want to wait for an arranged marriage like Angelina, then yes. But, if you want to have fun, I agree with Helen, ask him out!" Siobhan said.

"I think I will just let things happen naturally," Rose answered them all with an added wave of her hand.

Siobhan crossed her arms, "What about inviting him to that Jazz club your cousin took you to?"

"Billy's?" Rose shook her head, "No, that would be too much pressure."

"Then invite us," Helen interjected. "I have always wanted to go there."

Siobhan sat up higher in her seat, "That's a great idea! Let's do it. Do you think your cousin would take us?"

Rose shrugged her shoulders, "I don't see why not. When do you want to go?"

"How 'bout tonight?" Helen suggested. "It's Friday so we don't have to worry about being tired for tomorrow?"

"I don't know," Angelina debated.

"What don't you know?" Siobhan teased. "Either we all go, or none of us goes."

Siobhan was the reason that Angelina did anything socially. She encouraged Angelina to go to movies, shows, and restaurants. She did it in part because she wanted her friend to have a good time, but she also did it because her mother was more comfortable with her going out with a female friend.

"Fine," Angelina acquiesced.

* * *

By seven-thirty the four girls were stepping out of a cab and onto the sidewalk where the same crowd congregated the first night Rose arrived at Billy's. Rose recognized many of the same faces and greeted new ones with a smile and a nod. Rose even surprised herself how comfortable she became with coming to Billy's, although she never ventured to try whiskey for a second time.

Joe stepped around a couple of guys who were talking as they rested against the side of the building, "Rose, you made it!"

Joe greeted Rose with a kiss on her cheek and tipped his hat to her friends, "I am Rose's cousin Joe!" Rose could smell the sweet sting of whiskey on Joe's breath and giggled at his crooked smile and flushed cheeks.

"This is Helen, Siobhan, and Angelina," Rose introduced each of her friends.

"This way ladies," Joe chaperoned the four women inside the small club that was bursting with sound and motion. Patrons danced on the floor as the band played along to the melodic voice of Georgina Evans.

Angelina hung close to Siobhan who didn't hesitate as she walked into the club that was hazy with smoke. Helen tossed her coat and purse on the bench at the table Joe reserved for them and pulled Siobhan to the floor. Angelina slid in beside Rose and the two girls watched in awe as Siobhan and Helen bravely tackled the crowd with their dance moves. When the song ended, and the band moved to a slower beat, Siobhan and Helen returned to the table to have a drink and join Rose and Angelina.

Helen ordered a round of whiskeys for them, which Angelina and Rose were quick to refuse.

"What is the band's name?" Siobhan asked over the noise in the club.

Rose shook her head, "I don't think there is a name. Usually, the players change up sometimes, but the singer is Georgina Evans. Isn't she marvelous!"

"Absolutely," Helen exclaimed, "and so glamourous too!"

"She reminds me of Josephine Baker," Angelina said.

"That's right, I almost forgot when she came into the hotel when it opened," Siobhan said.

"You saw Josephine Baker!" Rose exclaimed.

"Saw her?! We met her!" Helen bragged.

Rose slapped her hands to the side of her face, "What?"

"She came for the opening of the hotel and had a specially reserved suite, or maybe a couple of them, I am not sure. And the whole time she was there she was flanked by tens of people and was constantly being stopped by guests in the hall. She never once hushed anyone away or refused an autograph for a fan." Siobhan explained.

"She is the most elegant and glamourous woman I think has ever graced the hotel," Angelina remembered,

"If I could have one night of being anyone it would be Josephine Baker."

"I heard she was a spy," Helen said.

"I don't think so, Helen. Why would she bother with that when she has it all wrapped up being a star!" Siobhan added.

"I read she is huge in France," Rose said, remembering the article she read in one of the magazines Mrs. Twindle had delivered.

Regardless of Miss Baker's rumored espionage activities, all four agreed that the beauty and talent of Ms. Baker were going to be remembered for generations to come.

Joe returned to the table to deliver another round of drinks when the band broke into another tune.

Helen's face dropped and she turned to face Rose, "Do you know what song this is?"

Rose shook her head.

"It's Beautiful Ohio," Helen slapped her hand on Rose's shoulder, "by Henry Burr! Don't tell me you never heard it?"

Again, Rose shook her head.

As if on cue, all four girls hoped up from the table and ran to the dance floor. As they all danced to the tune pointing at Rose, Helen and Siobhan belted out the words singing along, completely out of tune. As Rose began to move to the music, her body took over. It was a sense of freedom she never knew she could feel. Free from expectations, rules, or condemning eyes of people she grew up with. Inside the club, it was another world, one without pre-determined views of who you should be or who you should associate with. For the brief moments on the dance floor, Rose was suspended and time stood still, or at least it moved in a different direction.

Amid the laughter and dancing, the girls were oblivious to anyone around them. The lights of the club abruptly flashed on, and a sudden bang of the front door swinging open brought the band to an unexpected stop.

A young man ran towards the back of the building yelling, "Cops!" and burst through the door behind the stage, presumably into the back lane.

Everyone looked towards the door and watched as three policemen quickly made their way into the club shouting at the band to stop playing and for everyone to stay put. The band stopped playing, however, people began to push and shove their way towards the various exits from the club.

"Come on let's go," Joe suddenly appeared and grabbed Rose's elbow and shouted for the girls to follow him into the back. They ran over the top of the stage, clutching Georgina's hand as he passed. They cut a quick left and ran down the back hall. Joe pushed open the black steel door at the end of the hall and shoved the five girls ahead of him and then he quickly followed them to the exterior door at the other end of the room. Joe pushed it open and they began to run down the back lane and didn't stop until Joe called that they were far enough away.

Joe rested his hands on his knees and forced a steady breath into his lungs. After a few minutes, the heavy breaths turned into a burst of combined raucous laughter.

"That was incredible!" Siobhan yelled into the night air.

"A little too close for me!" Angelina exclaimed but still smiling.

Siobhan placed her hand on Angelina's shoulder, "You survived, didn't you?"

Joe led the girls around the corner, and they flagged a couple of cabs to the curb. Helen, Siobhan, and Angelina got into one cab, and Joe, Rose, and Georgina climbed into another.

The cab traveled through the dark streets in a direction that Rose was unfamiliar with. The lights of the cab shone on buildings that were like the ones around Joe's apartment, but the surrounding streets were new to Rose. The car stopped at a reddish brick walk up and Joe leaned into the driver and told him to wait. Without a word to Rose, Joe stepped out of the car and with his hand around Georgina's waist, walked up the front stairs to the building. Rose watched as it was Joe, not Georgina that pulled the key out and unlocked the door. Together they walked inside and disappeared for only a few minutes until the door reopened and Joe came bouncing down the steps.

He pulled open the door to the cab and slid onto the seat beside Rose and gave the driver the address of his apartment in Brooklyn. "What a night, huh, Rose?" Joe was beaming ear to ear.

"Definitely one for the books," Rose murmured. She wanted to ask Joe about Georgina but when she thought about it, it was none of her business who Joe spent his time with. And anyway, Georgina was wonderful and anytime Joe was around her he seemed the happiest he ever was.

As they drove, memories of the Jazz Club melted into the evening air, and with each block further from Billy's and closer to Brooklyn, the sound became more distant and dulled to a pounding in her head. The notes slowly faded and the haze of the smoke and sweet scent of whiskey grew distant too. But one thing remained strong. The feeling of freedom and Rose knew she had to return.

When they arrived home Joe and Rose climbed the stairs to the apartment and quietly unlocked the door and stepped inside. Rose turned to hug Joe and thanked him for everything that evening.

Joe offered the bathroom to Rose first so she could wash, brush her teeth, and set her hair for bed, as he learned she did every night. She struggled against her exhaustion to slip into her nightdress and pull the covers back on the bed.

She crawled into the cool cotton sheets and tucked the cover around her body. Rose stared out the window and watched the lights from the city as they danced above the buildings far away from Brooklyn.

With each blink, Rose drifted further into a deepening slumber and dreamed of the new excitement of her life. And as she sang the words to Beautiful Ohio in her head, she drifted off to a deep liberating slumber.

10

A beam of light crawled across the covers of Rose's sheets and warmed the top of her hand where it lay on her chest. She awoke to a clear blue sky and the aroma of coffee and breakfast cooking in the next room. Joe had been up early to see if he could repair some of the damage caused by last night's raid. He usually spoke in code when talking about his work, and Rose learned to understand that he was referring to the possible loss of his gin from the club. Joe kept some revealing signs of his paid activities around the apartment; however, unless Rose had been aware of the tools of which to distill alcohol, she never would have known. Joe; however, kept his business activities in a discreet location in a warehouse, and Rose respected his privacy and never asked where it was.

"I need to head out today to get some business cleared up. You have any plans for today?" Joe asked as he wiped his hands on a cloth before placing a plate of bacon and eggs on the table for Rose.

"I am going to go to the market and pick some things up for the week," Rose had planned all week long to spend the day shopping for some items that she missed having and would remind her of home, along with some food for Joe's place. They couldn't possibly continue to eat out every evening or subsist on coffee and bacon, which Rose was learning was top of Joe's meal repertoire.

Joe left and after Rose finished breakfast she quickly dressed and left for the market. Joe gave Rose exact instructions on how to get into town to do some shopping.

It didn't take long for Rose to notice the stark difference in the market experience in New York compared to her weekly visits to the local market and stores in Clarington. Her memory of the open market with freshly picked tomatoes still sweet off the vine and the dusty dryness of potatoes and beets were not going to be rekindled in the market in New York. Rose ran her fingers through the barrel of potatoes that were too small to have been picked properly and were absent of any scent or remnants of a farm. She used to marvel at her mother who would find the produce with a slight bruise that often brought a discount to her shopping list. Here, Rose found none of that familiar comradery.

Rose ventured over to a table of baked bread and treats and she fought back tears as the memories of being home began to flash into her mind. The sweetness of the baked bread and honey buns handmade by Mr. Lewison, whose cheeks bore a permanent rose color from hours at the oven, invited customers from several stands away.

But most of all Rose missed her mother's homemade soaps. Sprinkled with flecks of lavender and oats and, her sister Lily's favorite, the rosemary blended with cranberry zest. It offered Rose and her sisters a luxury that their family had no chance of affording. Rose would work alongside her mother as they prepared batches of soap for the family and wait impatiently the almost six weeks curing time it would take for the soaps to harden. Those were the memories that were hard to replace and impossible to forget.

But here in the New York market, rows of stalls lined the stores with wrapped produce dull from their travels from where they had grown and placed alongside the manufactured goods that were absent of the pleasures of nature.

Predominantly, Rose missed the friendly chatter in the market among the stalls. Children were gossiped about over a barrel of peaches, weather predictions bantered about next to the cider, and even Mrs. Twindle droning on about how much better the bread was in France (where she never had traveled to), and Mr. Lewison forcing a polite nod and smile as Mrs. Twindle picked over his treats, which she eventually would purchase anyway.

Rose walked a few blocks north and found a quiet park with a vacant bench and she calmly took a seat. A large elm tree grew behind the bench and stretched into the sky and over her head offering a full canopy of shade no matter the position of the sun. Rose leaned down to her bag and removed a small sketch pad she had stuffed in the side just before she left the apartment.

Rose could often be found drawing in her notebook in Clarington. Her sisters used to tease her, while Robert used to beam and admire her talent. He would sit quietly by her side, sometimes for hours, as she sketched various things around her. God, how she missed Robert. Tears filled her eyes and began to spill over her bottom lid and trickle down her cheek. A drop landed on the blank page of the sketch pad that sat open on Rose's lap. She watched as the water from her tear was slowly absorbed into the paper and spread into an uneven circle and left the spot wrinkled on the page.

That is how she was feeling here in New York. Like she didn't quite fill the page or fit in. She wanted to, but she didn't know how. Rose wiped the tears from her cheeks with the back of her hands and wondered if she should just return to Clarington where a planned life was waiting for her. One she didn't have to think about or plan. No surprises or anything new to get used to.

That's when a smile crossed her face as the thought of dancing with her new-found friends at Billy's just before the police burst through the door, and Peter's assertion that she is a New Yorker because she was brave enough to come in the first place. Rose knew that she couldn't leave. Not yet.

Rose pulled out her pencil and began to sketch her journey from Clarington. Recording her trip on the train, remembering the exhausted porter and the thankful look that crossed his face when she revealed one, small, light bag. She sketched the buildings around where she sat, working in detail every brick and ornate finishing on the edge of the building and around the windows. She watched a mother sit and read while her children played on the grass just a few feet from where she read. And Rose sketched them. She tried to capture the beauty of Georgina's singing but was only able to sketch the beauty of her face. The haze filled club that kept freedom so securely locked and waiting for the next time Rose went dancing.

Rose sketched Robert, but this time he was sitting at the edge of the water in the harbor looking onto New

York. Rose liked the thought of Robert watching over her.

She then took the most time to sketch her friends, and with the perfection of stroke captured Siobhan's free spirit, Angelina's reserved comfort, and Helen's wild imagination. When Rose was finished, she closed her sketch pad and noticed the sun was soon going to set for the day.

Rose's attention was drawn to raised voices that came from across the street. Rose watched from where she sat on the bench buffered with the protection of distance between them.

For most of the afternoon the woman, not far in age from Rose, waved loose pamphlets in her hand trying to encourage a few people to take one. Some did and walked on quickly after folding it into their pockets. Promising her they would read it in the privacy of their homes. Others eagerly took hold of the pamphlets and spoke a few kind words of encouragement to the woman before continuing with their day. Some flung vile words or stones in her direction accusing her of blasphemy and rotting the core of family values.

But mostly she was ignored. People walking past with not even an acknowledgment or an eye glance in her direction. People swerved around her as if she were an inanimate object. She stepped side to side trying to draw their attention to her cause.

Rose finally got up the nerve and decided to approach the woman across the street. She slipped her drawing pad and pencil into her bag and walked across the freshly manicured lawn, past the late blooms' fragrant aroma, and into the street where the warmth of the day radiated from the pavement.

The woman caught sight of Rose's movement towards her and locked eyes and smiled as it became obvious Rose was heading in her direction.

"Are you a sister interested in the women's movement?" She asked with a smile as she extended her arm towards Rose.

Rose nodded and reached for the pamphlet, her fingers were barely around the tip of the paper when a hand reached out from the left side of Rose's body and snapped the pamphlet from reach.

"Don't fall victim to these troublemakers Miss Farnsworth, if you know what's good for you!" Ms. Miller shoved the pamphlet back into the woman's hand.

"It *is* for her good," the woman responded calmly, "and yours as well." She held onto the pamphlet but kept her hand outstretched hoping that Rose would try once more to take the information.

Before Rose could make the decision, Ms. Miller grabbed hold of Rose's elbow and without another word to the woman, led Rose along the sidewalk away from the temptation of knowledge.

"You will do well, Miss Farnsworth to stay away from those sorts."

"Their organization is offering help to women. How can that be bad?" Rose felt braver on the open streets of the city speaking her mind to Ms. Miller than she would have been in the privacy of her office at the hotel.

There was a security in the open that Rose never felt before.

"How can that be bad?" Ms. Miller repeated Rose's question in a mocking tone. Rose was starting to dislike it when she did that.

"You'll get lured in with false promises but, the whole fabric of our society will be at risk of losing the thing that allowed us to strengthen and rebuild after the war. We owe our success and security to the very institution that these groups threaten to tear down."

Ms. Miller reminded Rose of the loyalty and the values of the hotel that she represents even when she is not working. When she felt she had imparted that importance upon Rose, Ms. Miller continued along her intended route.

Rose waited until Ms. Miller had turned the corner and was far enough away that Rose felt she was securely out of sight. But the time had passed for the opportunity for Rose to approach the woman for another pamphlet.

For as Rose watched from the far end of the street, the young woman promoting peace and liberty was being escorted away by a policeman. While a crowd hurled insults as she was led away.

For Rose the need to understand was strong. The woman would return to her familiar spot and as Rose headed home, she was determined that she too would return for the pamphlet.

With resolved motion, Rose tucked her bag under her arm and made her way back to the market to purchase some unappealing fruits and vegetables and make the best of what was to offer. And while she was there, she was going to find some lavender and oats, even if it killed her.

11

The buzz of excitement had been building for the whole week as the staff bustled about the hotel getting ready for the weekend performance in the Café Rouge. The hotel secured the booking of the country's most popular band over many other hotels in New York that were bidding for the event. The band was booked to perform Saturday evening in the Café Rouge and Mr. Statler ordered it closed for two days before their arrival to prepare the room for the lavish affair. It was rumored around the hotel (through only the most reliable of staff) that Mr. Statler won a bet with Mr. Aberthorpe J. Carberry, the most reclusive business magnate in New York, that he would not be able to sign the band to play at the Hotel Pennsylvania. Figures varied as to the amount of the wager; however, it was of little surprise to anyone who worked for Mr. Statler that he took the impossible challenge and worked until he was able to secure the deal. Even if it cost him more than the winning wager to do so.

As she walked into the hotel through the staff entrance, Rose found her blood was pumping in anticipation for the performance that was going to unfold in just a few short hours. Throughout the week, the staff was heard begging Ms. Miller for the opportunity to work on Saturday when they hoped they would be able to catch a glimpse of the band's leader, Mickey Hughes. Some even said they would work for free just to have an opportunity to be in the building at the same moment. Because of Ms. Miller's cold demeanor, she intentionally wouldn't book staff members who asked to work, specifically to ensure 'complete professionalism' in the hotel.

Siobhan, being more attuned to Ms. Miller's ways, told everyone to stay quiet about working and they would have a better shot to be staffed to work the Saturday night that Mickey Hughes and The New Jersey Revival were booked to perform.

When Rose arrived for work, she found Siobhan hiding behind one of the ornate marble columns that towered in the lobby as Mickey Hughes and his two bandmates were being checked into their rooms by the hotel manager.

Rose poked her in the shoulder. Siobhan gasped with shock and turned and faced Rose, and then quickly shot her a rueful grin, "What 'ya do that for?" Rose leaned in next to Siobhan and together they spied the entourage that, along with the band, were being registered at the front desk.

"I can't believe Mickey Hughes is just a few feet away!" Siobhan's voice quaked with excitement and her fair skin revealed her blush that extended from deep beyond the collar of her uniform.

Mickey Hughes was the possessor of many young hearts in the country. He was just shy of six feet and commanded the room just with his presence. He had the kind of face that made you stop and stare. His face had a comfortable, relaxed look that made every girl want to fall into his arms. His light, olive complexion ran smoothly over his perfectly sculptured cheekbones and around his angled jawline and disappeared under his starched collar that flared out over a charcoal plaid jacket. His vest did little to disguise his muscular build and trim form, but if Rose had to choose one feature that stood out it would be his eyes. Mickey Hughes' eyes were a deep, mesmerizing cerulean blue that held a warm, but serious expression. Even looking at him in a photograph caused a shiver to run up the length of your spine. His hair, a dark auburn, accented his handsome features, and the tousled manner he styled his hair gave him a playful bad boy look that every girl in America was attracted to.

"Have you ever seen anyone so handsome?" Siobhan asked Rose, not expecting an answer.

However, if Rose were to answer she would have informed Siobhan that Robert was the most handsome man she knew; instead, she stayed silent and just nodded in agreement.

Rose watched as a slim blonde woman sauntered up beside Mickey Hughes and slipped her gloved hand in his slightly bent elbow, and realized who it was, "Oh my! Do you know who that is Siobhan?" Rose slapped her hand over her mouth to keep from squealing with excitement.

Siobhan held a blank look on her face as she waited for Rose to enlighten her.

"That's Essie Stewart!" Rose often read stories about her in the magazines that came for Mrs. Twindle. Rose was impressed with Essie Stewart and everything she did. Her stardom on film was nothing compared to the waves she was making for women in America. She was an outspoken woman who believed she, along with all the other women in the country, had a right to be heard and to have a say in what was happening in the world. She was born Esther Stewart to Jewish immigrants and changed her name to Essie when she started acting. Never one to shy away from controversy, she was often seen at late night parties and in the arms of famous handsome men, like Jake Banks, Eric Strong, and now, Mickey Hughes.

"Oh, I have heard of her!" Siobhan exclaimed. "I heard she was working as a spy for the government."

Rose shot Siobhan a sideways glance and narrowed her eyes, "Where did you hear that?"

Siobhan stood straight and shoved her fists against her hips, "Around somewhere. But it's true. She uses her charm and stardom to get up close and personal with some pretty important businessmen when she travels to Europe. Especially when she was in France over the last few years."

Rose shrugged her shoulders, "Who knows."

A look of shock ran across Siobhan's face and she began to frantically pat Rose's shoulder, "Look!"

Rose looked in the direction Siobhan was looking and saw Mickey Hughes, with Essie Stewart on his arm, and his whole entourage walking towards where they stood hidden as they made their way towards the elevator banks. They didn't have time to run, so instead, Rose and Siobhan stood in place and blushed as they shyly tilted their heads down, only allowing their eyes to roll up and catch a glimpse of the entrancing group as they walked past.

Mickey Hughes was a few inches away and Rose fought the urge to reach out and touch him as he passed. He nodded and winked at them as they stood blushing by the ornate marble column. Siobhan grabbed hold of Rose's arm and dug her fingers into her skin to fight from screaming. As Essie Stewart walked past, a gentle scent of bergamot and jasmine trailed behind leaving a scant reminder she was there.

Rose held her breath until they were gone, and the elevator doors closed behind them.

* * *

Rose and Siobhan ran through the doors to the laundry room and broke out into a tangle of words as Angelina stood dumbfounded trying to make sense of what they were saying.

Siobhan slammed her hands on the stainless-steel laundry table sending an echo through the cavernous room, "Mickey Hughes is even more handsome in person!"

Angelina dropped the pile of towels she was carrying to a cart, "You saw him?!"

"And we even got a wink," Siobhan teased.

"I can't believe how close we were," Rose added. "You could even smell Essie's perfume!"

"What would have been great is to get to work the Café Rouge tonight instead of just in this laundry room, locked away from all the excitement," Siobhan complained.

"It's too bad you missed seeing them Angelina," Rose said, to which Angelina quickly turned around and lowered herself and began picking up the towels she dropped earlier.

"Angelina? What's wrong?" Rose asked.

Angelina stood up and placed the towels on the table in front of her and looked sheepishly at her two friends.

"Oh, I know that look Angelina," Siobhan said, "what did you do?"

Angelina slowly dipped her hands into her side pocket and pulled out a small blue and white package that had been hidden crumpled inside. As she dropped it to the table Siobhan and Rose saw the writing on the side of the package and a confused look ran across their faces as they read the label.

"Laxatives?" Siobhan asked.

Just then Ms. Miller burst through the doors, her face even tenser than it normally was and her scowl narrowed to a dangerous point, "You three," Ms. Miller pointed to Rose and her two friends shaking her long boney finger at them, "you all need to work tonight. It's an emergency and we are now short-staffed in the Café Rouge."

"What happened?" Rose asked.

"The cocktail waitresses that were slotted to work have all come down with some sort of stomach bug and have spent the entire morning in the women's bathroom."

Rose shot a sideways glance at Angelina.

Siobhan strained her smile as to not let her excitement show, "What is it you need us to do Ms. Miller?"

"Stand in the corner and hold some trays of drinks," she snapped, "Do you think you can handle that?"

The three nodded.

Ms. Miller gave a deep sigh, "Pick up your uniforms at four o'clock from the manager, and don't be late."

Ms. Miller turned around and placed her hand on the exit door and then twisted her body to face Rose, "And don't screw it up."

Rose watched as Ms. Miller pushed her way out of the door and listened as she stomped her way down the hall.

Rose and Siobhan turned to Angelina, who by now, had returned the damning evidence to her pocket and shot them a playful grin, and said, "You can thank me later."

To which they did, several times in fact, as they were getting into the uniforms provided to them by the manager. After a quick rundown of their duties by the much more pleasant Mr. Morrow, Rose followed Siobhan and Angelina into the Café Rouge. If the other staff were as impressed with the room as Rose was, they did a terrific job of concealing it. Rose stood, open-mouthed, as took in the splendor of the room as she entered it for the first time. The three distinct sections inside the room teased Rose's imagination as to the lavish parties and dinners that were thrown here regularly. She watched the waiters buzzing about the two terraced sections that sat on either end of the room. They hurried about laying crisp white linens and perfect arrangements of white flowers, which she knew to be Essie Stewart's favorite, and wondered if it was a coincidence or if Mickey Hughes had made the request as a condition of his performing here tonight.

The artificial limestone walls absorbed and warmed the lighting that cascaded from ornate fixtures on the ceiling and through wall sconces. Rose tried but couldn't make out the designs that were carved into the large wooden beams twenty-two feet above the floor.

The central focus this evening; however, was going to be the large area allocated for the New Jersey Revival on the central floor of the room.

Rose; however, was more attracted to the large floor-to-ceiling water fountain that sat on the east wall of the room. She walked over to the fountain and tried to memorize each feature and design so she could try and capture it later in her sketch pad. This must be something she needs to show her mother.

"I didn't know you were working tonight?" Rose turned and was standing face to face with Peter. Instantly a warmth rose in her cheeks as she caught his eyes.

"Yes, apparently some girls that were staffed to work tonight came down with a stomach bug," Rose smiled slightly at Angelina's surprising deviousness in securing them a spot in the room tonight.

Peter nodded, "Yeah, everyone is talking about that. Too bad."

"What are you doing here tonight?" Rose asked, eager to change the topic, and too nervous to think about what else to say.

"Same as you, serving drinks," Peter turned to look at the fountain. "This is beautiful isn't it?"

"Very."

A distinct clapping was heard coming from the middle of the room, "People! People! Everyone get ready, we will be opening the doors in ten minutes." Mr. Morrow began to get the staff in place and nervously smoothed the front of his jacket as he prepared to swing open the large doors and welcome in the throngs of excited guests.

It was exactly like Rose remembered from the pages of the magazines Mrs. Twindle had delivered and that she would secretly read in the back of Mr. Burrow's shop. For the remainder of the evening, Rose studied the clothes, hair, and movements of the myriad of magnificent guests that gathered in the Café Rouge to listen to Mickey Hughes and the New Jersey Revival play.

Occasionally Rose would catch a glimpse of Peter and wonder what he was really like. She watched how comfortably he spoke with guests and how well he worked alongside Mr. Morrow. When approached by Mr. Statler, he smiled comfortably and then rushed to attend to whatever request was thrown upon him by the imposing owner of the hotel. Peter's confidence and professionalism were evident to anyone who may have stopped to watch him. At one point in the evening, Peter caught Rose watching him and he smiled and nodded his head as he handed glasses of champagne to a table of elegantly dressed women, all giggling and joking with him while he worked.

The excitement really began when Mickey Hughes began to sing about thirty minutes after the doors first opened.

The three members of the New Jersey Revival arranged themselves on stage and as the drummer began to start a beat, the trumpet player began to play and the deep, creamy voice of Mickey Hughes quickly filled the large room. Unlike the thick haze that was unavoidable in Billy's club, the Café Rouge's large size dispersed the smoke and the band was easily visible from every corner of the room. The crowd eagerly moved to the energetic beat that vaulted from the instruments. Those that remained seated quickly joined in with the rhythmic tapping of their feet under the linen-covered tables. Servers nodded their heads in beat with the band as they carried themselves around the room replacing empty glasses of whiskey or champagne, ensuring the libations of the crowd did not wane.

The notes rose from where the band played and filled the room until not one person was left untouched by the powerful effect that Mickey Hughes could have on each person he played in front of. It was more than music for Mickey Hughes. Both the crowd and he were transfixed by the rhythm that poured out of him, surging through the crowd until they were unable to ignore it. As she watched him on stage, Rose believed Mickey Hughes could have sung all night long.

The evening eventually ended, and after the crowd left and the New Jersey Revival departed along with their entourage in tow, the night staff began the tiring task of clearing the room.

Rose returned her uniform and was pulling on her coat when she heard drunken giggles come from around the corner in the hall. Rose ducked behind a post not wanting the stray guests to see her when she realized the sound of the voice was that of Helen. Rose peeked as a man, much older than Helen, nuzzled his face in the crook of her neck and with his arms wrapped around her waist pulled her in close to his body. The sound of hushed giggles and voices was followed by the rustling of a key from the man's pocket. Rose watched as Helen swung the man's hotel key in front of his face and together, they slipped around the corner and headed for the back exit of the lobby.

Once Rose was sure the hall was clear she left the hotel hoping she wasn't too far behind Siobhan and Angelina. Rose stepped out onto the crowded sidewalk and twisted her head from side to side but could not see Siobhan or Angelina. They must have left without her and now she would have to make her way home alone.

Just as she was wondering if she was brave enough to walk in the dark alone, a familiar voice spoke up behind her, "Can I walk you home?"

Rose breathed a sigh of relief when Peter made the offer. She gladly accepted explaining that she had never been out by herself so late in the city.

"No problem," Peter extended his left arm inviting Rose to walk ahead of him in that direction. "I don't mind, I quite like being out so late in New York anyway."

Rose blushed as Peter placed his hand on the middle of her back and steered her around a crowd laughing and chatting on the sidewalk near the road.

"Plus," Peter added, "It will give me a chance to chat to you more."

Together they walked south for over an hour and Rose was surprised how easy it was to speak with Peter. She hadn't felt this comfortable with anyone since Robert died.

"So why did you come to New York?" it was a question that Rose had been asked frequently since arriving. She was always vague when answering and before she was too shy to be completely honest with Peter. Until tonight. Before tonight their conversations hung on information about the city or food or movies. Everything superficial and safe.

But tonight, was different. Rose spoke to Peter so naturally and shared her heartbreaking experience with Robert right through to the terrifying suggestion of marriage to Ernest Russell. The conversation spilled out of Rose freely and without tears, as she shared her mix of fear and excitement of starting a new life so far away from home.

Peter listened patiently, never interrupting Rose and knowing when to nod, smile, or place a gentle hand on her shoulder.

"It sounds like you did the right thing, if you ask me," Peter suddenly pulled Rose across the street to where they began to walk towards the bridge.

Rose couldn't believe how far they had walked, and now they were crossing the bridge into Brooklyn.

"You sound like you are from here," Rose said, guiding the conversation away from her.

"Actually," Peter began with a giggle. "I am from Italy."

The confession took Rose by surprise, "Peter Albert does not sound Italian."

"Pietro Alberti does."

"Yes, it does!" Rose laughed, "Why did you change your name?"

Peter moved his head from side to side and shrugged his shoulders, "I guess I just thought it was easier to fit in at first."

"And now?" Rose asked more seriously.

"Now I am used to being Peter Albert."

"Pietro Alberti!" Rose announced loudly into the night air, with the flair of an Italian accent that she picked up joking around with Angelina. "I like that."

Peter's hand brushed against Rose's and in harmony, they reached out and wrapped their fingers together. They walked the last half hour and Peter shared his dream of starting his own restaurant in New York and was hoping to get the experience he needed while working at the hotel.

"And the money of course," Peter added.

Rose stopped when they reached her building, "This is it." Rose pointed to the brick walkup where she lived with Joe.

They stood in silence for a few minutes, neither one wanting the evening to end. Peter squeezed Rose's hand and moved his face closer to hers. When he looked into her eyes, it was like every breath in Rose's lungs was still and she was unable to move. The sound of her heart pulsed against her ears and she fought the urge to pull him close to her.

He leaned in slowly and placed his lips against the side of her cheek, never letting go of her hand. Rose stood transfixed by the feeling of his skin against hers and willed it to last forever.

Rose stayed silent as Peter pulled back and smiled.

He stood on the sidewalk as Rose climbed the steps to the apartment and waited there until she closed the door behind her.

Rose watched through the apartment window as Peter slipped his hands into his pockets and walked back in the same direction that they came from.

That night, as Rose lay in bed, she traced the outline of his lips with her memory and felt a fullness in her soul that did not exist before. This is what falling in love was like and she didn't want it to end.

12

The beating lasted only twenty minutes. But it was long enough to inflict the right amount of pain. The thud of Joe's body being thrown against the apartment door echoed loudly through the silent apartment. Rose had been asleep for three hours when the bang, followed by pounding steps descending from their landing, had awoken her from a deep sleep.

Rose hurried as she pulled her robe over her shoulders and ran out of her room. Disoriented, Rose made her way towards the lamp and flung her hand towards the switch sending it crashing to the floor. She fumbled with the second lamp and this time managed to switch it on.

Moans and a week knock came from the hall just on the other side of the door.

"Joe!" Rose yelled, not sure if she even expected a response.

Another loud moan, full of pain emanated from the other side of the door.

Rose slid the chain from the lock and released the handle. As Rose pulled the door open, Joe's slumped and beaten body spilled into the apartment.

Rose lifted his face and ran her hand along the side of his jaw and tried to rouse him to consciousness.

She peered into the hall, and once she was sure there was no sign of his attacker, Rose slipped her hands under Joe's arms and dragged him into the apartment. Once he was fully inside, Rose slammed the door shut and quickly turned the lock and pulled the chain across the upper bar, just in case the men who dropped Joe at the door decided to return.

The dim light from the lamp cascaded a shadow over the left side of Joe's face shielding the full extent of the battering he suffered. His right eye had already begun to swell shut and a cut on his lip stretched open revealing the white tendon under his cheek.

Joe moaned each time Rose shifted and moved his body into place until she finally got him lifted onto the sofa. He settled his head against the back of the wall and breathed out a deep sigh.

"Joe, what happened?" Rose asked.

Joe chuckled, then coughed in pain and grabbed his ribs, "A competitor of mine." And that was enough of an explanation for Rose.

Joe was sent a stark reminder that he could be brought down at any moment, but that never deterred him. His dream was to build an empire with his special recipe of gin. He was positive that one day it would become legal to sell stronger alcohol. He just had to hold on.

The police were in every body's pocket – those that succumbed to the pressure that is – and eventually, most did. It was the only way anyone could stay in business.

For those that paid, they would receive notification of planned raids by officers, giving everyone time to evacuate and hide any illegal alcohol on the premises.

Quick flip bar tops and hidden basement holding tanks along with tunnels and secret passageways that led out of buildings and into back lanes or hidden rooms.

Joe had protection and paid dearly to the cops that along with the trust he built with his clients would inoculate him from the violent competition. Tomorrow Joe promised that revenge would be enacted, and things set right.

Joe reassured Rose that there was a rhythm to how things worked in the city. And as Joe explained it more clearly to her, she understood that the undercurrent of the city could exist if it never threatened to cross into the pristine landscape of everyday lives in New York.

Then it occurred to Rose that her life straddled those two worlds.

13

Monday came faster than expected and Rose was eager to get to work early with some hope that she would see Peter before her shift. A storm had hit the city starting Sunday evening, and the rain hadn't let up all night. Rose ran the distance from the train to the hotel holding her bag over her head trying in vain to shield herself from the downpour. Shaking the rain from her coat, she stepped through the staff entrance and walked towards the laundry room.

"Miss Farnsworth," Rose turned at the sound of Ms. Miller's voice and she silently cursed her poor timing.

However, Rose forced a smile as she answered, "Yes, Ms. Miller."

"How would you like to fill in for one of our chambermaids today?"

The surprising offer was friendly and enticing; however, the look on Ms. Miller's face made Rose feel like it was more like a punishment.

Nevertheless, Rose was eager to accept the offer and became quickly aware that she had not been trained for the job. Siobhan rescued Rose with a quick rundown of the tasks that were expected of a chambermaid and assured her that she would be fine.

Many reservations had been canceled due to the storm and Rose was solely responsible for arranging the rooms on the seventeenth floor for the guests due to arrive later in the week.

Rose was halfway through the rooms on the seventeenth floor when she had to return to the supply room to gather more towels. As she was returning to the staff elevator, the bellhop called to her just as the brass doors were closing.

"Can you take this up to room 1783?" the bellhop held an evening gown shrouded in wrap fresh from Macy's.

Rose took the gown and stepped into the elevator just before it closed.

Room 1783 was at the northeast corner of the building and as she made her way down the hall, Rose was becoming more comfortable with the layout of the hotel and it was feeling more familiar every day.

Rose tapped three short times, and when she did not get a response, she inserted the chambermaid key in the lock and opened the door. One of the features of the hotel was that no two rooms were exactly alike, giving the guests a new experience every time they stayed there.

Rose carried the wrapped gown and hung it in the closet. Rose ran her fingers gently over the fashionable outfits that were already in the closet. Her fingers slid over the silky fabrics and sent a shiver up her spine as she imagined slipping one of them over her shoulders. Below the gowns, five pairs of shoes were perfectly placed. Each shoe a different color than the one before and a slightly different design, and above the gowns on the shelf sat five purses. One to match each pair of shoes.

Rose bent down and lifted the red leather shoe that caught her eye above all the others. She unbuckled the strap and wiggled her foot out of her shoe before slipping it inside. Instantly she transported herself to the stage where Georgina Evans stood singing, or to the dance floor where Essie Stewart entranced Mickey Hughes as she swayed her body to the sound of his voice.

Reluctantly, Rose returned the shoe to the closet and closed the door shut.

Drawn by the elegance of the hotel guest's clothes, Rose grew more curious. She moved around the room glancing at the magazines that lay at the end of the bed and on the table near the window. Recent editions of the same magazines Mrs. Twindle ordered, and Rose lived vicariously through and that she read in secret in the back of Mr. Burrow's shop. On the cover of the magazine near the bedside table was a picture of Essie Stewart. She wore her hair pinned up with a fashionable feather band. Her head was tossed back, mid-laugh, and the string of pearls around her neck were caught by the photographer as they were sliding off her elegant shoulder. Immediately Rose remembered the magic of that night and her late-night walk home with Peter.

She continued to dream as, for a moment, she dove into the captivating life of this mysterious but elegant hotel guest.

On the dressing table, Rose spotted an array of cosmetics. Lip stain and blush that was quickly becoming all the rage and a bottle of pump perfume, possibly even purchased in Paris. A red velvet tassel with a tuft of gold thread hung from the top and draped around the base of the amber bottle and was marked with writing Rose did not recognize.

To the left of the bottle was a pamphlet folded closed, but still visible through the glass bottle. It was the same pamphlet the woman tried to give Rose and Ms. Miller stopped her from taking. Rose lifted the pamphlet and read the front cover. Women's Freedom League was written across the top in newspaper font and a sketch of a woman throwing out an apron and holding up a sign was displayed on the front.

Inside the pamphlet outlined not only the suffragette movement but the ability for women to work after they married, and to even have the right to appropriate health care and control the timing of their pregnancies.

The sound of a laugh from the hall aroused Rose from her daydream and she quickly returned the pamphlet to the table and hurried towards the door. When she stepped into the hall, she ran straight into the bellhop who was returning from room 1785 after delivering trunks of luggage.

"What are you doing?" he snapped at Rose.

"Bringing the gown up just like you asked," she explained.

He slapped his hand to his forehead, "You are supposed to put it in here." With a frustrated look, he pointed at the four-foot-high, concave feature in the center of the room's door. "It's called a Servidor, and that's where we put things like that. Shoes, clothes that are to be delivered to the room for the guest. It gives them their privacy."

Together they quickly unlocked the door to the room, retrieved the dress and he showed Rose how to place the gown in the Servidor by unlocking it from the hall.

"See," the bellhop said.

Rose thanked him and knew if Ms. Miller were to become aware of her misstep, she would have been sacked immediately.

The remainder of the day passed without any disruption and Rose, feeling lifted by the day, walked the long-distance home. The rain had lifted, and the sun quickly warmed the streets.

Rose bounced up the stairs of the building and when she reached the landing a pair of feet jutted out from the railing above her. She ran the last flight of stairs and screamed.

"Joe!"

There, tossed like a forgotten bag, Joe once again lay crumpled against the base of the door. Rose shook his shoulders as she shouted his name. As she rolled him over, he began to groan in pain.

His right eye was swollen over with a deep purple patch and blood had dried on the corner of his mouth. The left side of his face bore scrapes that looked as if he had been dragged across the pavement for a distance. Rose stopped shaking him for fear she would hurt him further, and she began to gently pat his shoulder.

"Joe, wake up!" she repeated until his groans turned into coughs and he began to awaken.

After a bit of a struggle, Rose helped Joe to his feet and into the apartment. Once inside she lay him on the couch and grabbed a cloth from the icebox and placed it on his eye. Without asking, Rose grabbed a glass and a bottle from the secret panel under his sink and poured him a drink.

"I didn't know you knew where that was?" Joe laughed and then quickly winced at the pain in his ribs.

Rose held out the glass of amber liquid for Joe, "Who do you think has been cleaning this place?" She sat across from her cousin and waited for an explanation. When one didn't come, she began to ask what happened.

"Nothing you need to worry about Rose," Joe waved his left hand in the air and then took a swig of his drink, draining the glass.

Rose quickly surveyed Joe's visible injuries, while trying not to stare at his face. His nose was bloodied and had started to bleed after she lifted Joe from the floor. The angle of his nose was off, and she was sure it had been broken. Joe sat motionless, with his eyes fixed on the door. Rose's bottom lip began to quiver, and tears rolled down her face and Joe realized Rose was truly and deeply afraid.

He placed his left hand on top of hers and told her not to worry.

Tears ran down her cheeks and she wiped them with the back of her hand, "How can I not worry! I thought you were dead! What if I was here by myself?"

It was easy to forget that Rose was seventeen and had moved from Clarington not long ago. She adjusted so easily and never complained about being homesick or fearful of the big change. Joe knew he owed her an explanation.

"I had a disagreement with a business associate," Joe explained, "They wouldn't have hurt you. I promise."

"How do you know?"

"Because they make too much money from me and need to keep me alive. This," Joe pointed to his face, "was a way of reminding me that they are still there."

"I am calling the police Joe," Rose began to stand, and Joe grabbed her wrist.

"You can't," he snapped.

"Give me one good reason why?" Rose challenged.

"Because it was a copper who did this to me. Okay. So just leave it."

Rose sat dumbfounded, staring at Joe's bloodied face, and shocked at the idea that a policeman did this to him.

Rose put most of the pieces together of what Joe did for 'work' and knew that he ran an illegal liquor distributing company, supplying underground as well as legal clubs in the state. He produced a special blend of gin that was not available through legal channels and at a better price. The catch, Joe explained, was that slipping a few cops some cash now and again kept raids to a minimum and promised to keep him out of jail.

Joe was trying to break free of the arrangement and was faced with some resistance in the process.

After another drink and some aspirin, Joe excused himself for the rest of the evening and left Rose to eat alone that night.

Later, as Rose lay in her bed, she realized that the undercurrent of the city was closer than she thought, and the allure of a better life could easily be tainted by greed and power.

14

Weeks had passed and so too did the bruises on Joe's face. The familiar spark that shone in Joe's eyes began to return, especially when he was around Georgina. Georgina came around to the apartment more freely to see Joe since neighbors began to think she was there to see Rose. Rose enjoyed Georgina's visits and the chats she would have with her. She was a woman with worldly advice that had been pinned down by the expectations of society and she fought hard to succeed. Falling in love with Joe was just one more hurdle she said. It reminded Rose of how she felt in Clarington, with her life being planned for her since the day she was born.

Rose had started to go to Billy's a little more often with Siobhan and Angelina. Helen came less and less as she became more enamored with the older men that would send attention her way.

"She should be careful," Siobhan circled her hand in a swooping motion over her stomach.

"You don't think she's..." Rose leaned forward to whisper over the table, "pregnant."

"I hope not. Especially since there is no need for it," Siobhan explained.

"What do you mean?" Rose asked.

Angelina rolled her eyes knowing the conversation that was going to follow.

"There are methods available for women to make sure that they don't get pregnant."

"Like what?" Rose asked, then remembered the pamphlet she read.

Siobhan began to explain the different forms of birth control that were becoming available to women.

"The clinic is not too far from where I live. It's been around for about three years now and even though there is no sign, word has spread enough to let women know about it."

"There are that many single women who need it?" Rose blushed slightly as she thought about the reasons why someone would use birth control.

"Single women. Married women." Siobhan explained.

"Married women?"

"Look, it's a new age, Rose. Married women don't want to be held down by kids if they are not ready. There are a lot of people not happy about it. It gives us a lot of power to start to have control over our bodies. Plus, it beats the alternative."

Rose looked inquisitively at her friends.

And Siobhan explained about the mishaps when women would go to back-alley doctors that promised to fix their situation only to find out they had an infection or worse, some would die.

Rose was too shy to ask if either of her friends had used any of the methods, but if she had to guess, she would have said Siobhan was more familiar than Angelina.

Siobhan had started to date Angelina's brother, Sam, not long after the evening Mikey Hughes performed at the Café Rouge. Sam had arrived at the hotel to walk Angelina home because of the late hour. Siobhan, who was also leaving the hotel, walked with them and Angelina said the two of them never took their eyes off each other. Ever since then, Rose kept her personal questions about Siobhan's dating life out of earshot of Angelina. But tonight, the three girls promised to have a night just for themselves and they agreed it was far too long since they had been dancing.

Billy's was exceptionally busy, and the haze of the smoke became more familiar and comforting every time Rose came. The room was filled with many unfamiliar faces that were jammed in amongst the familiar ones.

Strangers congregated between tables and along the bar. Some leaning against the walls in the back of the club as they rested between songs.

Billy was making his way over to her table as Siobhan and Angelina were returning from the dancefloor and left three drinks. One whiskey and two sodas.

Even though the night was planned for the three friends, Siobhan invited a girl she met at one of her Women's Freedom meetings. She was in town studying at the university and from out of the country.

"I remember what it was like being from out of the country and new to the city so I thought it would be nice to ask her along," Siobhan explained.

"Where is she from?" Angelina asked.

"You can ask her yourself," Siobhan pointed to the door. "There she is now." Siobhan stood and waved her arm to the slender woman who walked through the door.

She was fashionably dressed and had a short bob that hung to the middle of her neck. Glasses wrapped around her face, but you could easily see her green eyes and a wide smile from across the room. She quickly walked over to where they were sitting and pulled off her coat when she was at the table.

"You made it!" Siobhan exclaimed, and then ordered a drink for her with a wave of her hand to Billy.

"I finished my paper earlier than I thought."

"These are my friends," Siobhan pointed first at Rose then at Angelina as she introduced them.

"Pleased to meet you all. My name is Eileen. Glad to meet you," the new friend eagerly and confidently stretched out her hand to each of the girls at the table and then took a seat.

"Siobhan said you are from out of the country. Where are you from?" Angelina asked.

"I am here studying Art at Columbia University," Eileen explained. "I am from Canada."

"Canada? Where?" Rose asked.

"Winnipeg."

Only Siobhan had heard of it, which didn't surprise either Rose or Angelina.

"I have a cousin that emigrated to Canada and works for the railway up there. I have never been though." Siobhan proudly explained.

Angelina was more curious about the fact that Eileen was studying at Columbia University. "Are there many girls at University?"

"More since the number of men enrolling dropped because of the war. But not enough as far as I am concerned."

Eileen went on to explain how she was one of five children, with only one child being a male. Ironically, he was the only one to not go to university. "He ended up working with our father in the family printing business instead. The rest of us got the opportunity to travel and get educated."

Angelina peppered Eileen with questions and by the time the evening was over Eileen and she had exchanged addresses and promised to stay in touch. Rose had never seen such life or interest in Angelina since she met her on that first day she came to the hotel.

As Rose listened, she heard Angelina talk about her dream of becoming a teacher and maybe even traveling out west to venture into a warmer climate and a new path. As she spoke and Eileen asked questions as to why she never did it, a sadness crossed Angelina's face as she explained it just wasn't something that any girl in her family would be encouraged to do. Plus, the finances were too great to undertake. Watching Angelina struggle with the loss of her dreams reminded Rose of the day she buried Robert and thought all her dreams were over. Rose put a supportive arm around Angelina's shoulder and encouraged her friend that she could do it.

The girls agreed and together they continued to reassure Angelina that she could fulfill her dream and promised to help her devise a plan. Whether it was the resounding encouragement from their conversation or the exhilaration from the music that infected the crowd,

Angelina grew stronger and more adamant about taking the next step in her life.

The girls walked a long distance before they flagged a cab. While they walked Angelina talked nonstop and it was evident something was sparked in her that evening after meeting Eileen.

"Do you know she was the president of her university student group last year? She was the first woman ever to be elected. And she is not just studying Art, she is studying for her Masters! Can you believe it?"

Angelina was losing herself in a new space in the world she didn't know could exist until tonight. The idea of a woman being able to pursue an education at a higher level was not just something foreign to most women of their generation, but specifically to Angelina's family who expected her to be married and have started a family by now.

The world was opening to all of them in New York in 1919, but maybe most of all to Angelina who was on the cusp of a new beginning.

15

The problem with women getting a taste of freedoms is that invariable complexities develop. This was the predominant thinking and feeling of those set in their ways of the comfort of a predictable life. What shocked Rose wasn't that this type of thinking existed, lord knows it was the type of thinking that blanketed the small town she was raised in. What surprised Rose was the large number of women who voiced their opinions against any advancement of women. Siobhan guessed it had more to do with the connection that type of thinking held with reproductive rights and the conflict with their religious beliefs. And Rose felt that some voiced their objections publicly to appease their husbands but privately they felt differently. This was clear when Rose spotted three women who she had seen harassing the woman on the street handing out pamphlets, seated at the front of the room waiting for the meeting to start.

Emily Blankshift gathered up her papers and headed towards the front of the room and hoisted herself up on the raised podium and dropped her sheets on the flat hollow surface as she called the meeting to order.

The Banks Hotel was the originally planned location for the Women's Freedom Group. That is until the hotel manager grew uncomfortable with explaining to the businessmen who frequently stayed at the hotel that there would be no unrest with the gathering. After several threats to pull their business, The Banks Hotel regretted to inform the women that they would be unable to host the gathering after all.

Rose had wondered how The Hotel Pennsylvania would have dealt with the swelling controversy.

Instead of gathering in the lushly carpeted, floral wallpapered room at The Banks Hotel, Rose found herself in the basement of a church hall in the middle of an area of the city known as Hell's Kitchen.

The lights were sparingly used, as were the use of cleaning products Rose surmised as she glanced at the dirt-stained floors and grime-covered windows. There were attendees wrapped in silk and wearing expensive jewels and pearls gathered along with an assortment of women from different classes and different parts of town amongst the dank forgotten space. Not unlike how they were forgotten in society.

Rose read the pain and unease on the faces of some of the women in the room, who in another setting, would have displayed their wealth as a sign of pride. Tonight, Rose almost thought they looked as if they dressed to try and mask their ability to have a say in the direction of their lives. Women held many scars and unknowingly carried them forward from one generation to another and were unfortunately used to masking their desires. And Rose thought of the life that was planned out for her back home. Before she was able to speak, and then when she could, decisions were made without her say.

Rose looked around the room and was hit with a wave of dampness in the air. Rose waved her hand in front of her face hoping it would move some stale air away and fresh air towards her nose. The scent of Parisian perfume morphed with the damp mold and threatened to settle permanently in Rose's new wool wrap, and she instantly regretted wearing it tonight.

Emily began the meeting slowly and then not long into the night many voices from the crowd erupted with cries of displeasure that had been suppressed most, if not all, of their lives. Stories were shared and some women cried, but all there tonight agreed they had something worth winning. The question was how they were going to go about it.

Violence appealed to no one and beyond that ideas were few.

Emily opened the floor up to anyone who may have ideas or plans, and the room fell silent. After a few minutes a woman who was seated at the front of the room stood, and without turning around to face the crowd, began to speak. "I work hard. Two jobs if I can get them. To feed my family. I clean the houses you live in and make the food you eat in your fancy restaurants. But I am nobody in this country. First to the wealthy women in this room. Second to anyone in the city or country. How could we have come together to fight for our country in the war to preserve our freedom, and then return to this?! A system that is broken and unfair. So, if we are going to fight for a change it has to be together or it won't hold."

People shot awkward glances at each other. Those with pearled necks, wrapped their coats tighter around their shoulders to hide their jewels.

The woman continued, "Maybe if we win it will be better and we won't feel separated by who we know and what we have. Or maybe we will win, but nothing will change between us. I don't know. But isn't it worth trying? Isn't the risk and effort worth the prize?"

Silence fell upon the room as the unknown woman lowered herself in her seat and waited for others to speak up and voice their opinion. Some had brought up the idea of a peaceful march in many different parts of town to help build their numbers. One woman offered to travel to Washington where she could speak with a distant cousin of hers who worked in government, hoping it may open a door for them.

The madness of the early part of the evening faded and the wealthy looked like the poor, the poor looked like the wealthy and all looked towards Emily Blankshift for the sign on how to proceed. Over the next week, the women in the room planned their approach.

16

The group bustled with excitement as they rushed to the front of the line as the train was beginning to board passengers. Joe had arranged for Rose and her friends to join him and his friends for a weekend on the New Jersey boardwalk. The stipulation being that Georgina needed to register under a room with Rose and her friends. The crew scrambled along the platform in eager anticipation for their time at the beach. Rose had seen pictures and heard stories about the crowds of people that gathered along the boardwalk and congregated on the beach.

Rose and her friends purchased matching outfits that were suitable for the beach, but comfortable enough in the heat. Siobhan purchased a large brimmed hat to go along with her outfit providing her with a wide sphere of shade throughout the whole day.

If the ride out on the train was any indication of the time they would have in New Jersey, it was sure to be a marvelous weekend. Joe's friends charmed every young woman who was traveling without a chaperone, and most had the good sense to turn them away. Especially Siobhan who was knee-deep in love with Angelina's brother Sam.

The chatter on the train sped up as the train pulled into the station and slowed to a stop. Everyone grabbed their bags and rushed towards the exit and clamored to reach the boardwalk before they registered at the hotels.

The beach ran as far as Rose could see along the unending stretch of water. Crowds of people mingled on the sand, some playing catch and others walking and chatting. Rose's eye was drawn to the few swimming in the water and watched with envy as they jumped into the rolling waves laughing.

Joe pulled Rose's elbow, "Come on, let's check-in. I want to show you everything along the boardwalk."

The group walked into the lobby and headed straight for the front desk. The front desk clerk at The Penn had a friend that worked at The Jersey Hotel that was situated on the boardwalk and offered to call ahead and make sure they had a set of rooms with a view.

"Wow, Bessie wasn't kidding when she said her friend could get us a great room," Siobhan rushed to the window and marveled at the view of the water and crowds of people below.

After a quick change, the girls hurried to meet Joe on the boardwalk in front of the hotel.

People walked along the boardwalk chatting and laughing. Some arm in arm, others chasing after children who ran ahead a little too far. Rose giggled at the sight of the men in their swimsuits as they rushed in and out of the waves while their wives looked on. There was a real mix of ages along the shoreline. What struck Rose is the complete comfort and enjoyment everyone seemed to be having.

White painted covered carts carrying travelers were pushed along the boardwalk by young men who gleefully transported people from one area of the boardwalk to another. Joe walked as he chatted with his friends and Rose admired how he looked in his fashionable light-colored suit. Georgina wore a soft peach beach dress and sported a matching hat that was wrapped fashionably with a soft cream ribbon. Angelina and Rose opted to walk without a hat as they enjoyed the warmth of the sun on their face and did not have any fear of burning, unlike Siobhan, who compensated by wearing a hat with an extra-wide brim.

After an hour of sightseeing, Joe grabbed hold of Georgina's arm and promised Rose to be back before dinner when he had reserved a table for them at Rodney's, a supper club on the boardwalk. Rose watched as Joe and Georgina walked ahead and her heart filled with love for her cousin and she hoped that he and Georgina would find a way to be happy. And that Joe would find a way to be safe.

Siobhan and Angelina grew tired and returned to the hotel to lay down for a while before joining everyone for dinner.

After Rose convinced Siobhan and Angelina that she would be safe walking alone, they returned to the hotel to lay down for a nap before joining everyone for dinner. Rose was thankful for the peace and she quickly found a large rock among a break wall that sat between an area off the boardwalk and between the water.

Rose kicked off her shoes and hopped up on the closest rock and jumped over the spaces between until she reached the middle of the clump and she sat down and removed her sketch pad from her bag. Rose had sketched in her pad every evening since that day in the park when she decided to turn her attitude around about New York. In it, she captured what she thought the essence of New York was.

She was spending more time with Peter every week and she looked forward to the days they planned on the weekends when they would walk around the city exploring. He introduced her to parts of the city she would never have known about and they experienced food, music and they shared dreams of what their future would hold.

The most difficult sketch was the one she was trying to finish of him. She would find herself halfway through when she would stop and start again, feeling she didn't quite capture his eyes correctly. Today; however, she focused on the crowds of people frolicking on the beach not far from where she sat. She was so deeply entranced in her drawing that she almost didn't hear her name being called from behind her.

She turned around to see Peter slipping off his shoes and walking over the same large rocks she did until he reached where she sat sketching.

"I didn't know you were coming here this weekend?" Peter gleefully asked.

"Joe arranged for a bunch of us to come out. What are you doing here?"

"My Aunt and Uncle own a restaurant on the strip and now and again I come and help them out. You should swing by and check it out."

Rose promised to stop by before she returned to the city. She felt flustered in Peter's presence and fought the blush that forced its way to her cheeks.

Rose was eager to share her excitement of the day with Peter. They looked out into the water and were captivated by the change in the sky's hue as the sun began to set. They sat quietly like that for quite some time after talking.

Peter gently placed his hand next to hers on the rock but was too nervous to hold her hand, somehow exposed here in public on the beach. Rose lost count of how many stones they tossed into the sand in front of them. It was a distraction for them both to shield their nervousness as they spoke. It started slowly but before too long they had tossed hundreds of stones and shared both the important and vague things in their lives.

At times Rose's thoughts were jumbled, as she forced herself to focus on Peter but was constantly distracted by his soothing voice and the gaze of his peaceful eyes.

Peter reached down to grab another stone and his hand brushed on top of hers. A tingling sensation reverberated through her whole body and caught her off guard. They gazed at each other long enough for Rose to relax as Peter leaned in and gently kissed her.

An all at once, they both knew they had found their soul mates and that New York had given Rose her greatest gift. As Rose leaned in closer, everything around her fell away and she felt happier and more secure than she ever had in her whole life.

17

By the time the train was ready to leave on Sunday afternoon, Rose had already made plans to return to New Jersey with her friends for another weekend. The complete freedom and release she felt were intoxicating and she was unable to imagine not coming back. Peter had joined them for dinner on Saturday evening and Joe had given his seal of approval, as did her friends for the match between them. Rose blushed at the sound of her and Peter as a couple and grew shy when her friends spoke of him.

"You'll have to write home to Auntie Dot and let her know all about him," Joe teased. But Rose knew all too soon she would have to do just that if she were to plan a life with him. Which lately she found herself happily dreaming about.

Rose was exhausted from the trip back to Brooklyn and when they walked into the apartment, she dropped her bag in her room and flopped down on the couch. Joe walked in behind her and as he stepped inside his foot kicked a telegram that had been slipped under the door while they were away.

Joe sliced open the envelope and began to quietly read it as Rose nestled in by the arm of the couch pulling her feet up under her. She noticed a concerned look across Joe's face and she sat up straight.

"What's wrong Joe?" she asked.

He held up the paper that he pulled from the envelope, "It's from your mother. Your father is sick, and she wants you to return home."

She was pretty good at hiding her feelings when she knew she needed to. Now; however, was not one of those times. As Rose felt the searing pull of being dragged underwater with each word Joe read from the telegram, a look of fear crossed her face. Not for the fate of her father, but for the loss of her freedom.

18

Keeping her breakfast down was proving to be harder than Rose anticipated. Mixed feelings clouded Rose's mind and heart as she traveled the long distance back to Clarington. Through tears, she broke the news to Peter who held her close and rubbed her back until she calmed down. She knew he thought she was sad because of the news of her father and she was too embarrassed to say it was her selfish need to stay in New York that affected her more deeply. Rose loved her father, but the command he held over the first seventeen years of her life seemed quite enough to sacrifice to him. He was all too eager to marry her off to Ernest Russell, whom he knew to be an angry drunk.

If anything was learned during the time she spent in New York, it was that there was more to life than she was raised to hope for, and she was afraid to let it go.

Rose struggled to decide what to pack, and in the end, she packed the same outfits she originally traveled to New York with. Each time she selected a new dress or outfit she had purchased while in New York she was flooded with fears her mother would not approve and quickly returned them to her closet. Except for one outfit.

Rose chose a smart suit she purchased on sale a month ago and decided to wear it as her travel suit. The charcoal grey was fashionable, would hide any wrinkles from traveling and, if need be, it would suffice for an outfit for a funeral.

Rose immediately chastised herself for even thinking about her father dying.

The train arrived on time and her sister Lily was waiting on the platform with her husband Raymond. Lily nervously tapped her foot and tugged at Raymond's arm as she scanned the windows of the train cars looking for Rose. Rose called out to Lily when she stepped from the train and Lily quickly ran towards her with tears flowing from her eyes.

Rose held her sister as she tried to explain through sobs about what happened to their father, as their mother's telegram was somewhat vague.

Raymond placed his large hand on Lily's shoulder and leaned in to hug Rose. He calmly explained that their father had had an attack while working in the field. He was alone, so there is some speculation as to exactly what happened, but the doctor thinks it was his heart.

Lily wiped the tears from her eyes and smiled at Rose, "At least you're here. You can take care of things better than any of us."

Rose cringed at the implication of her assumption. Lily was unaware of Rose's discomfort, but Raymond was too keen to not notice and too kind to mention it.

Rose's imagination played various scenarios in her head as to what she should expect when she walked in the door of their family home. Ultimately, she decided to be prepared for the worst and expect her father to be completely incapacitated upon her arrival.

Her mother was waiting at the base of the steps to their front porch (still layered with peeling paint) and stood with her hands clasped together at her chest when she saw Rose arrive with Raymond and Lily. She ran to her daughter and grabbed hold of her for the first time since she left.

"I wasn't sure I would ever see you again Rose," her mother whispered in her ear.

"I wasn't sure I would ever return," Rose confessed only to herself.

Her mother walked her inside and Rose was instantly hit with the aromas that conjured up memories of her youth, only the way an old family home can. Each home held its own personality, its own history, and especially its own scent.

Rose had never realized it when she lived here but their home smelled of warm pine and sweet bread. They were never a wealthy family, but it occurred to Rose that her parents always made sure they had a good home, clothes to wear, and food to eat. Guilt welled up in her throat and choked the tears to her eyes. Filled with selfishness for her new life, she never imagined how she could have been happy in Clarington. She convinced herself that to be free to enjoy the happiness in New York it had to be balanced with some discontent from her past.

She went to her parent's room where her father lay recuperating in bed. She walked quietly into the room and felt an unexpected swell of love as she saw her once strong and independent father lay frail and helpless under the wool blanket her mother had tucked tightly around his thin body.

Whether he heard her footsteps or sensed her presence, Frank Farnsworth opened his eyes the moment his daughter walked in the room. A weak, but a distinct smile crossed his pale face as he looked upon Rose standing in the doorway.

"A fever has kept him in bed the last few days, but the doctor says he should be right as rain in no time," Rose's mother walked into the room behind her carrying a cup of tea and set it on the table next to the bed.

Frank tapped the bed and motioned for Rose to come close to where he lay, "Let me get a good look at you Rose." His voice was weak but warm.

How could she have forgotten that?

Rose grabbed hold of his hand and sat on the edge of the bed. For a half-hour Rose told her father about the exciting things in New York, at least the things she knew he would be comfortable with. Things like the architecture of the buildings and bridges, the trains and subways. Things she experienced but never threatened to reveal her true passion in the city. The people and the social change that was stirring up the city and especially her generation. So, therefore, she decided to leave out Billy's club, Joe's beating, and all the social advancements for women that would surely cause her father to worry further.

After some time, Rose stood and insisted her father get some rest and she assured him she would be staying until he was better. She sat until he drifted off and his deep rhythmic breathing assured her that he was asleep.

She also forced her mother to take a cup of tea in her chair by the fireplace and to relax until she returned. She would see to dinner and help figure out what they would do next.

Rose left the house when her sister wasn't watching and tread quietly down the peeling front steps. She started to walk the quarter-mile into town, and along the way had hoped she could sort out some things in her mind. She kicked rocks absentmindedly as she made her way towards Mr. Burrow's shop, just as she did as a child.

The store hadn't changed since she left, although Rose didn't know why she would have thought it would have. She hadn't been gone that long and businesses in Clarington just seemed to plod along. They were businesses of need not of excess, and that kept them safe from changing fads. The dusty silence of the streets in Clarington was a stark reminder of the difference that New York had introduced into her life and now was her new normal.

Rose pulled the heavy door to the feed store open and stepped inside as the bell that was hanging on the hinge rang.

Mr. Burrows turned to greet his customer, and then a look of surprise covered his face, "Rose!"

He walked towards her as fast as he was able and gave her a warm hug, "I am so sorry to hear about your father." He then grabbed hold of her shoulders and looked her in the eyes with warm sympathy, "That must be why you are back, dear." He said. Rose wanted to tell him how right he was, but instead, she nodded in agreement, and then changed the topic. "I wanted to thank you for everything you did for me before I left."

Mr. Burrow stood straight and folded his arms across his chest and smiled, "You don't have to thank me. You were the best employee I have ever had."

Just as Mr. Burrow was extolling Rose's work virtues, a crash echoed from the back storeroom. Mr. Burrow, unflinching, rolled his eyes and shook his head, and pointed to the back of the store, "That is your replacement."

Rose giggled as Mary-Jane Gerber walked out from the storeroom and began to explain, "I am sorry Mr. Burrow. I tried to stack the boxes just as you asked, and they just tipped over!"

"Never mind...." Mr. Burrow waved his hands in the air and walked into the storeroom without uttering another word.

"Rose Farnsworth!" Mary-Jane yelped when she realized to whom Mr. Burrow was speaking.

Rose hugged her friend and asked her how she was doing, "Good. Outside of the storeroom challenges, that is."

Mary-Jane held up her left hand and displayed a thin band of gold, that if she had not pointed it out, Rose could have easily missed it. Rose grabbed her friend's hand and smiled, "Congratulations, Mary-Jane. Who is the lucky guy?"

"Ernie. Ernie Russell."

19

Rose stared in shock as Mary-Jane stood smiling as she revealed she was now Mrs. Ernest Russell. The look of joy that ran through Mary-Jane's voice and was revealed in her eyes was not the response she would have expected from someone who had married Ernest Russell. She experienced a suffocating fear just at the mention from her father that she should marry Ernie. But as Rose stood confused, Mary-Jane's joy became more evident as she explained the brief, but shocking courtship, that culminated in a quick wedding two months ago.

Mary-Jane tapped her lower belly, "Don't tell Mr. Burrow but I am not going to be here too much longer. If you know what I mean!"

"You're pregnant!" Rose asked, more shocked than jovial, and as soon as Rose was aware of her tone, she regretted it immediately. Luckily Mary-Jane was too enraptured with her news to notice.

She leaned in and whispered to Rose, "I just hope there aren't too many."

Rose hesitated, then said, "There are things you can do...you know, to prevent further children Mary-Jane." Rose explained.

"Rose! How could you...Ernie would be suspicious if I didn't come to him regularly." She admitted shyly.

"No, I mean there are other things," Rose said, "ways to prevent a pregnancy but still..." Rose motioned side to side with her hand the way Siobhan did when she spoke in code about sex.

Mary-Jane blushed, "I am not that kind of girl Rose! I am not sure what you are learning in New York, but you better not let your mother hear you speak like that."

And like that Rose was ten years old and being caught by Mrs. Graham for talking about kissing a boy. When she threatened to tell her parents, Rose ran the whole way home in tears. She spent the evening hiding in her room feigning illness and avoided her parents as much as she could until the end of the week when she was certain Mrs. Graham had not uttered a word to her mother. Rose finally realized Mrs. Graham would have then been forced to have a conversation that involved talking about a subject she spent her whole life avoiding.

Mary-Jane continued to talk incessantly about her new life with Ernie and all the plans they had, which were not unlike the plans the other new young wives had in town. Baby. House. Repeat. And Rose had all but tuned Mary-Jane's words out as she stood waiting for the perfect break to escape.

"...and Ernie has already begun to map out our new home and everything," Mary-Jane excitedly explained.

"New home?" Rose asked, "Aren't you staying with his parents. That's where..."

"That's where we were going to have to live." Rose was about to say but stopped herself mid-sentence.

"As soon as Ernie's parents knew we were thinking of marrying, they gave us the farm that they had owned his whole life. They wanted us to have a great new start. And as luck would have it, Ernie was able to get a big job supplying corn to a few manufacturing plants up north so that brought in a lot of money." Mary-Jane placed her hand over her smiling lips. "I wouldn't have said anything, except I am sure with you being up in New York and all, you must be used to seeing folks with a lot of money."

Rose smiled as Mary-Jane spoke but didn't know what to say.

Mary-Jane watched Rose's face remain unchanged and realized what may be going through her mind and was the one to break the silence. "I know what you may be thinking."

"What is that Mary-Jane?" Rose asked.

"Look, everyone in town knows how Ernie could be when he was drinking, but it's all changed now."

"How so?" Rose asked.

"I told Ernie if I was to date him that he was not going to be drunk all the time, and yelling and stuff," Mary-Jane folded her arms in front of her chest, "That was non-negotiable. My daddy wasn't going to let me marry a drunk and, let's face it, Rose, there weren't a lot of available men to go around."

Rose felt a stab of pain as she remembered the comfort of her planned life with Robert and suddenly missed Peter more than she thought she would.

Mary-Jane told Rose that Ernie had cleaned himself up, began working hard, "and he goes to church every Sunday and has not touched a drop since his promise."

Rose patiently waited as Mary-Jane spoke for a little while longer and then when the opportunity presented itself, she excused herself to return home.

Mary-Jane made Rose promise to come to visit with her before she left town again, and Rose did promise - even though she had no intention of doing so.

Rose quickened her pace as she left the store and headed back home down the same dusty road that took her into town.

At that moment, Rose felt a flash of anger that briefly shielded her from the pain she was feeling at remembering the planned life she had with Robert. The life that was unfairly stolen from them when he died. Tears continued to run down Rose's face as she walked along the road. The remorse that crept into Rose's heart became overwhelming as she felt she finally realized what really mattered was family.

A family that could be hers. And soon the regret mounted as Rose realized she did not learn that lesson soon enough to make a difference in her life.

20

Rose awoke from an uneasy sleep and thought to herself, as she stared at the ceiling, "I have really messed things up." Tears and self-doubt filled Rose since she had returned. She had noticed the stark difference between the two worlds in which she lived, and she found herself questioning her values, which she never had done before. She had transitioned so easily into a massively different way of life in New York that she wondered if she ever fit into life in Clarington before she left? Now she found herself wondering if she fit into life in New York because she was missing Robert and the idea of them starting a family. She questioned the truth of her love for Robert and wondered if it was a way for her to escape a life, one she didn't even know she didn't want. But in the end, she knew her feelings for Robert were pure and refused to punish his memory with her moments of insecurity. Her emotions and mind wandered from her previous life to her new life and realized that even though she was the same person living in those two lives, she didn't recognize either one.

Rose slipped out from the sheets and walked along the bare floor and grabbed the robe that lay across the top of the hope chest that still stood at the foot of her bed. Rose dropped her robe on the bed and bent down and lifted the lid of the chest, revealing the untouched items that lay inside. Rose's hands went directly to the small items of clothing that were intended for children. The children she was supposed to have with Robert. They had agreed if it was a girl that she would be called Sally. And if it was a boy, they agreed instantly that he would be called Andrew. Tears built in her eyes as she pulled each item out of the bottom of the chest and lay them across the floor in front of where she knelt. Rose ran her fingers over the cross-stitching along the front of the nightdress her mother sewed for the first child she hoped that Rose would have. Rose felt an emptiness in her gut, and she started to feel as if every decision she made since she left for New York was the wrong decision to make. She heard steps approach from the end of the hall and quickly returned the items to the hope chest and wiped the tears from her eyes. She pulled her robe over her shoulders and went to join her mother in the kitchen for breakfast, and hopefully come up with a plan on how to fix her life.

The evening before Rose was playing cards with her sisters and momentarily her life began to resemble the life she led before. The night was filled with laughter as each of them took turns sharing stories of their childhood. She was eager to share stories and moments from her life in New York as she had left so much out of the letters she wrote home, for fear of worrying her parents. The opportunity presented itself when Betty began to steer the conversation towards her new life.

She asked Rose what it was like in New York and Rose's smile instinctively stretched across her face reaching the furthest point it could. Rose gushed with excitement as she began to reveal the electricity that was alive every day in the hotel. The shining marble floors "so clear you could set your curls in them". Paintings that were too many to count and too ornate to describe in detail that would do them justice.

Rose explained in detail the evening that Mikey Hughes arrived to play the Café Rouge. Everything except Peter kissing her that night. The glamour and the excitement of the hotel held her sisters transfixed as she described in complete detail the music, food, even the scent of the flowers.

"Even in the cold of winter, they'll ship them in!" Rose exclaimed proudly as if she alone were responsible for them.

She saved the glamour of the people for the end and she watched as her sisters listened perched on the edge of each word hoping to fall into her reality, altogether forgetting about the cards.

Like an excited child stretched on tiptoes at the candy counter, Rose's sisters absorbed every detail she shared.

"Aren't you afraid of the city?" Ruth asked.

As Ruth asked the question, Rose could feel her mother's eyes glance sideways at the girls as they spoke. Rose remembered the excitement she felt the night Billy's was raided by the police and sent her and her friends running and laughing into the night.

"No," Rose answered.

"Sally told me her uncle said there are many women's groups that gather and riot in the streets," Betty said.

Rose felt anger rise in her as she remembered Ms. Miller's warning as she reprimanded her for wanting to take a pamphlet and subsequently that same woman being led away by a policeman. Then the impassioned speech was given by the unknown woman in the basement of the church hall in the middle of Hell's Kitchen that called all women to peaceful arms to fight for the right to 'be'.

But knowing her mother was listening she tempered her answer, as she tempered the information in her letters.

"It's not like that," Rose assured her sisters, and indirectly her mother. "They are peaceful groups that want to see the peaceful acceptance of all women into society and for them to have a say in the laws that affect them." Rose answered and then added, "Just like men do now."

A week had passed since Rose arrived back home and she began to settle into a set routine. Not unlike the routine she had before she left for New York. After dinner, Rose and her mother cleared the table and tidied the kitchen in silence. Lily helped Rose get her father ready for the long night of sleep, which was sure to come aided with Dr. Cliff's special tonic he prepared for their father. Her father was getting stronger every day; however, it was a slow progression back to good health. Dr. Cliff assured Rose that her father would be fine to return to his normal activities in a few months but that he should take care and not work long days anymore. Rose knew that was going to be easier said than done when it came time to convince her father but decided she would cross that bridge when it came time.

Rose was seated in her father's chair by the fireplace reading and her mother was sitting across from her working a cross stitch pattern for a dress she was making for the church fair. As with most evenings, they passed it in silence, each to their own thoughts and pastimes.

Rose could feel the stare from her mother's eyes, and she lowered her book and raised her head to face her, "What is it, mom? Is everything okay?"

Her mother strained a smile, but a look of worry revealed itself all too easily, "I am wondering what your plans are Rose?"

Rose closed her book, "My plans?"

Her mother nodded.

"Well, actually, now that you ask. I was in to speak to Mr. Burrow the other day about getting my job back. With Mary-Jane expecting a baby, he will need a replacement."

Her mother knew that Rose was feeling a fleeting regret at passing up the offer of marriage to Ernie and was second-guessing her move to New York. The announcement of Rose's plans to restart her life again where she left off out of some misplaced sense of loss caused Dorothy Farnsworth to stand in anger.

"Rose," her mother did not get angry often, but when she did, it was a secret to no one around. "I don't care how happy Mary-Jane is right now, it wasn't the life for you."

"How do you know that Mom?" Rose asked, tears beginning to glisten in her eyes. "I could have had a nice quiet life here. And I could be the one expecting a child, and here to help you with Dad."

Rose threw her hand over her face as the tears came hard and fast.

Rose's mother wrapped her arms around her daughter and tried her best to comfort her. In the end, she just held her until the tears subsided.

Rose wiped her eyes and sat back, "I just wish I hadn't gone to New York."

Dorothy brushed the hair back from Rose's damp face, "I have something to show you."

Dorothy left the room and returned a few minutes later with a black box securely held in her hands. Even from across the room, Rose could see the years of dust that layered on the top of the box. Dorothy sat in the chair across from Rose and exhaled a deep breath. She smiled at her daughter and Rose was sure she could see a flush in her mother's cheeks as she contemplated the contents of the box. Dorothy wiggled the lid from the box where it was tightly secured since before Rose was born. Sprinkles of dust floated to the floor with a few remaining specks that hovered in the air, haphazardly looking for a place to land.

Rose leaned forward and glanced in the box. She looked silently as her mother lifted a small book that was bound at the short end with string. The edges were frayed, and the corners turned up revealing years of use. Dorothy grabbed hold of the book with her slim fingers and carefully lifted it out of its dusty vault. She caressed the top of the book with her right hand and smiled just before she handed the book to Rose.

Without saying a word, Rose took the book from her mother and opened the faded green cover, and glanced at the first page. Rose continued to flip the pages and unknowingly revealed a deep secret from her mother's past. Each page was as marvelous as the one that preceded it.

Rose opened her mouth to speak and realized she had been holding her breath since her mother handed her the sketch pad, "I didn't know you were such a good artist?"

"Why do you think I took such an interest in your talent Rose?"

"I guess I just thought you were being a supportive parent," Rose continued to flip the pages in her mother's sketch pad. "These are remarkable, mom. How come you never showed us these before?"

In response, Dorothy reached into the box and pulled out a folded piece of paper and held it in her hand for a short moment before unfolding it and handing it to Rose.

Rose read the top band of text that ran across the heading of the page, "Ford's Vaudeville Theatre?" It was more of a question than a statement. Rose continued to read the sheet for some sort of indication of how this related to her mother but couldn't find one, except for the fact it was in Boston where her mother spent much of her youth.

"The theatre opened in '83 to rave reviews," Dorothy smiled at the memory she conjured up in her mind as she spoke. "It was an instant hit, much to the chagrin of older members of the community. Word quickly spread from town to town, and from businessmen and audience members that visited the city."

Rose waved the sheet in her hand, "But how does this relate to you?"

"I was one of the young actresses in the troupe," Dorothy pointed to one of the names typed across the bottom of the page. "Sadie Brown."

Rose laughed, "A stage name?"

Dorothy raised a hand to her mouth as she tried to quiet a laugh as she nodded, "Many actors and actresses used them. It wasn't uncommon. It was all part of the act really, and it had the added benefit of shielding my persona from my parents."

"What happened?" Rose asked.

"I met your father," Dorothy explained, and then quickly added. "Oh, it wasn't his fault. He didn't make me give it up, it was my choice. Your father was up in Boston selling grain to some buyers and after a successful week, one of the older men in the group invited your father and some of the younger guys to a show at the theatre."

Rose wanted to ask her mother what happened but stopped short and decided to let her go on.

Dorothy continued to explain, "It was love at first sight Rose. After one date I knew that your father was the one for me. He couldn't move up to Boston and continue his farming practice, so it was up to me to move to Clarington if we were going to be together."

"Did you ever regret your choice?" Rose wanted to know but was unsure she wanted to hear the answer.

Dorothy quickly shook her head, "No, I missed the theatre, but I never regretted the decision I made." Dorothy paused, "I love my life, Rose."

"Why are you showing me this now?" Rose asked.

Dorothy lowered the box to the ground, leaned forward, and grabbed hold of her daughter's hands, "Because I can see you are deciding to stay for the wrong reason. You can't stay here because you feel you missed something by leaving. That isn't fair to anyone, least of all to you."

"But you need me here now mom, especially with what happened to dad," Rose trailed off not feeling strong in her defense.

"I am fine. We are all fine. I can see more than anyone the fire that has ignited in you since you have been in New York. You need to follow your dream *there,* Rose. Once you lost Robert it opened another path for you to follow. He would have wanted you to continue to see it through. We all do."

Tears flowed uncontrollably from Rose's eyes, "But I am scared mom."

"Of what dear?" Dorothy stroked her daughter's head as she cried.

"Of missing out on a family, and happiness," Rose sobbed.

Dorothy gently touched Rose's chin and lifted her face, "One person's version of happiness does not mean it is going to be another's version of happiness. It also doesn't mean you won't find it in New York either?"

Rose fell into her mother's lap and sobbed as her mother rubbed her back.

"You need to go back Rose," her mother whispered in her ear.

Rose knew her mother was right, and before the evening was over Rose would admit it as well. Her life in Clarington was always going to be a part of her, but it had changed, and it was over, and she needed to be able to leave it behind if she was going to have a chance of a happy future in New York. When Rose packed her bag the next day, she took the dresses she brought from New York and wrapped her mother's sketch pad safely inside the pale blue scarf she bought at Macy's. It was the only thing she was bringing with her from Clarington. And this time she knew she wouldn't be back.

21

Rose awoke to a loud banging on the door of the apartment. At first, the noise was distant, as if in a dream, but when the placement of the banging didn't meld with her dream of the seashore Rose was pulled from her sleep. She stumbled from her bed missing the edge of the night table but colliding with the leg of her bed. Her toe throbbed as she grabbed hold of it and hopped out of her room and towards the sound. It was still dark outside, and Rose felt a sinking feeling of dread, remembering the last time she was awoken from deep sleep to find Joe severely beaten and dumped against the front door. She was quickly relieved when the light was switched on and she saw Joe stumble out of his room, looking as if he was equally in the depths of slumber.

"What do you think that is?" Rose mumbled through her tight sleepy throat.

Joe shrugged his shoulders, "Only one way to find out." And he proceeded to open the door. As he released the locks, he turned his head around and nodded towards Rose, "Your nightdress...."

Rose returned to her bedroom and pulled her robe from the hook on the back of the door as Joe opened the door. Siobhan flew into the apartment as soon as Joe released the last lock, nearly hitting Joe in the head with the side of the door.

Siobhan shook and was panting heavily as she tried to explain what caused her late-night visit.

Rose ran to comfort her friend forgetting about the pain in her foot and not noticing the small prints of blood she left on the floor with each step.

"What's wrong Siobhan?" Rose guided her to the sofa as Joe closed the door.

"It's Helen," she blurted out. "I don't know what to do?"

Siobhan looked from Rose to Joe then back to Rose again.

Helen had been seeing (she refused to use the word dated as it was too committal) Alexander for a few months and had as the girls expected become more physically involved.

Helen, being Helen, lived from one moment to the next narrowly missing any consequence that would normally befall girls in their day and age.

Now Helen had found she missed her monthly and realized this was a situation she could not wiggle out of by flashing a smile and batting her eyelashes. No extent of smiles and sweet-talking was going to make the reality of a baby fade.

Helen risked being sent back to Chicago, or worse if Father Donovan became aware of her pregnancy. Alexander wanted to marry Helen and had been asking her since their third date. He even carried a ring around in his pocket just in the event Helen said yes one day.

"I couldn't imagine being tied down to one man my whole life!" she would exclaim. "It would be dreadful."

"Even if you loved him?" Rose had asked one day.

"Especially if I loved him," Helen answered. "It would be so unfair to restrict him to one woman, especially if she didn't want to be there."

Now Siobhan was sitting in Rose's apartment at three in the morning on a Sunday, shaking with tears because Helen was now in a completely difficult situation and could see no way out.

As soon as Helen realized she was pregnant, and right after turning down another proposal from Alexander (who finally thought he had Helen in a position where she could not refuse him) she searched out a woman who promised "relief" from her predicament. The woman, Elise Kruger, practiced herbal medicine in the back room of a small storefront in the outskirts of Brooklyn. For the price of one month's salary and the agreement of secrecy, the two women risked being thrown in jail to gain control over Helen's life.

Helen took a mix of tansy, scotch broom, mugwort and yarrow, and a few other ingredients she couldn't pronounce or remember and was assured that after a few days of feeling ill she would be relieved of her situation.

Instead, Helen grew more ill with each passing hour and violent pains followed her convulsing sickness. Her fever spiked and continued to rise through the night.

"But why come here? You need to call a doctor." Rose said.

"She can't," Siobhan said.

"Why not?" Rose asked.

"Because they'll have to call the cops and she'll land in the slammer," Joe explained speaking for the first time since Siobhan pushed into the apartment.

"That's why I'm here," Siobhan explained and this time she looked directly at Joe.

Joe crossed his arms and looked at Siobhan, knowing exactly what she meant.

"I don't understand," Rose said.

Siobhan didn't turn her face from Joe's glance, "You know people, don't you Joe? That can help her?"

Rose listened on, confused, and aware she was no longer part of the conversation and that it was Joe who Siobhan needed tonight.

Joe stared at Siobhan and didn't answer.

"Please Joe! She'll die otherwise," Siobhan pleaded.

"Every time he helps someone, he risks getting arrested. Are you sure that Helen is in serious trouble?"

"Come see for yourself," Siobhan stood and walked towards Joe.

Joe sighed, nodded, and then said, "Let me get dressed."

Within minutes the three were running down the stairs to a waiting car.

"Who's that?" Joe asked nervously, not wanting to involve more people than necessary.

"Alexander," Siobhan quickly answered, "Please let's hurry."

Angelina was sitting with Helen in Alexander's apartment, trying her best to make her comfortable until help (hopefully) arrived.

Joe agreed once he saw Helen that she needed more help than a few aspirins and Angelina's cold cloths were offering.

Within half an hour Dr. Kinney was next to Helen and began to examine her.

A short while later he walked out of the bedroom dabbing his forehead with a cloth, and with news for Alexander.

"I gave her a course of antibiotics and something a little stronger for the pain," Dr. Kinney said.

"And the baby?" Alexander asked.

"Everything still seems intact. For now. Time will tell if she will lose it or not. The next forty-eight hours will let us know both Helen and the baby's fate. Until then, see she takes these at the prescribed intervals, and I will pop in to see her later today." Dr. Kinney handed Alexander two bottles of pills. One bottle with pale yellow pills and the other with small oval white pills, along with specific instructions for doses and times.

For the next two days, Helen drifted in and out of consciousness and reached varying degrees of fever. The girls all called in sick blaming the stomach flu for their absence and stayed by their friend's side. They each took turns cooling her forehead and changing her sheets and even taking to reading some passages from a few of Helen's favorite books. Even the ones that made Angelina blush.

Because that is what friends do. They are there. With no judgments or harsh words.

And all the while Alexander sat perched in a faded and torn club chair a short few inches from Helen's side. Stroking the side of her face and holding her hand.

He was a man who would give everything to her, and she a woman who would give nothing to him, for fear of losing her freedom.

Yet he stayed knowing he wasn't what she wanted but because it was what Helen needed. He was in love. Rose prayed it would be enough.

22

Rose was eager to return to New York and her work at the hotel; however, she had to survive the lecture from Ms. Miller as to the virtues of dependability and hard work, and the importance of loyalty for all employees. Rose stood erect and motionless for the full ten minutes that Ms. Miller spoke, not even giving in to the temptation to scratch an itch that was rising on the side of her nose. Rose was reminded of the importance of upholding the reputation of the hotel as it reflected directly on everyone who gave her the opportunity, including Mr. Statler as well as Ms. Miller herself. Rose began to blush uncontrollably as she felt she was being reprimanded for something she should be embarrassed about doing; however, she couldn't imagine what that could have been. She was about to begin to defend herself to Ms. Miller and remind her that she was just visiting her sick father but thought better of it and continued to receive the onslaught of Ms. Miller's lecture in silence. Once the lecture had ceased, Rose was quickly dismissed, and she wasted no time as she turned to leave Ms. Miller's office. Ms. Miller surprisingly gave herself a slight reprieve from her cold sternness and uttered, "I hope your father is on the mend" as Rose was leaving her office. Rose nodded in appreciation of the kind words but knew enough of Ms. Miller from her time at the hotel to know it wasn't an invitation for further conversation, and she gently closed the door.

Rose breathed a sigh of relief as she walked down the hall and her thoughts quickly turned to Peter. She hadn't seen him since she returned and had wanted to surprise him later today. Rose had suppressed her feelings for Peter. Either out of misplaced guilt of replacing Robert's love or out of fear it meant she would have to face taking a leap of faith and abandoning the comfortable avoidance of her feelings. No matter the reason, Rose quickly began to accept her love for Peter after her mother helped her to see that her future was no longer in Clarington, although it didn't have to be separate from it. Rose found it hard to rest on the train ride into New York as she recalled her time at the beach with Peter. Alone in the train car, Rose's cheeks flushed as she remembered their first kiss and how she felt as she watched him walk away from her apartment with a slight skip in his step.

"It seemed as if you survived Ms. Miller's lecture and see let you come back to work!!" Siobhan ran and hugged Rose just as the two were about to step into the laundry room. "Angelina finally left Alexander alone to be with Helen, so she returned yesterday," Siobhan's expression suddenly turned serious, "I never did ask you how your father was, with all the commotion and all with Helen."

Rose smiled and held her friend's hand, "He is much better, thank you."

Siobhan's carefree smile quickly returned, "Have you told Peter you are back?" Siobhan picked up on Rose's feelings towards Peter before even Rose was willing to admit it.

"Not yet," Rose replied. "I am going to surprise him later today. I have been so worried about Helen."

"Don't wait too long," Siobhan warned, "He's a real catch and won't last long."

The girls smiled as Siobhan pushed open the door to the laundry room and Rose followed behind. The following hours that occupied their morning work shift was bursting with the lighthearted banter that Rose didn't realize she needed or missed, and before too long they were sitting in the lunchroom eating a fruit salad.

"So how is Helen today?" Rose asked.

Both Siobhan and Angelina passed each other a short glance before they began to speak, making sure they were quiet enough to keep their conversation private.

"Helen didn't lose the baby Rose," Angelina leaned in as she began to speak.

"So, she is better then?" Rose asked.

Siobhan took a swig from her coffee cup and then put it on the table to the left of her and leaned into the center of the table, "Yes. But she cried for hours after she awoke. Some of the upset was because she was still pregnant, but I think she felt bad about being faced with the prospect of needing to marry Alexander! And as soon as Ms. Miller found out, she sacked her."

"I know she is upset but I think he'll be good for her. He confessed to me that he has no interest in suppressing Helen's spirit. He said it was what made him fall for her in the first place. I just hope she can accept him." Rose said.

"Helen is not the only one getting married," Angelina piped up.

Rose looked at Siobhan who placed her hand flat on the table and displayed her engagement ring.

Rose's jaw hung open.

Siobhan reached over and pushed Rose's chin up, "Don't make a scene, Ms. Miller is already watching all of us girls closely. After Helen got sacked, we were all dragged into her office, one at a time to be given a stern lecture of the virtues of young women working at the hotel and how any actions we take outside our working hours reflects directly on the hotel." Siobhan rolled her eyes, "Like she would know."

Rose began to understand the motivation in Ms. Miller's lecture, and how it had nothing to do with Rose directly, but everything to do with the situation that Helen found herself in now.

Angelina shoved Siobhan with her elbow, "This is serious. We could all be sacked just as quickly even if Ms. Miller just thought we did something she disapproved of."

"That seems so unfair," Rose whispered.

"I agree," Siobhan agreed. "She should have been better prepared, is all."

"She shouldn't have done it, is all," Angelina interjected.

"Did any of the fellows get the same lecture?" Rose asked both her friends, to which they responded with a look of surprise.

"No, why?" Angelina asked.

"Well, it does take two. If I remember my mother's speech correctly," Rose said.

Siobhan smacked her hand on the table, "That is so true! Why are we women always being pulled in and given the business?"

"It is just the way it is, I guess," Angelina said.

"Well, it shouldn't be. It's just not right," Rose stuck a fork in a small cherry and popped it into her mouth. The next few minutes the three ate in silence.

Rose was the first to break the quiet when she asked, "What did you mean Siobhan when you said Helen should have been prepared?"

"You know, with birth control," she said.

Rose blushed and looked blankly at Siobhan.

"Don't tell me you haven't heard of birth control?"

"I have heard of it," Rose defended her naivety. "I just don't know how she could have been prepared?"

"There's a clinic in Brooklyn called Brently, and it's where they help women who want to avoid becoming pregnant."

"Who goes there?" Rose asked.

"All sorts of women. Rich ones that stay here," Siobhan waved her hand in the air indicating the hotel, "women with too many mouths to feed and girls like us."

Rose quickly reddened at the inclusion of herself in the group of women who would have visited the Brooklyn clinic, and instantly she was ashamed at feeling embarrassed. After all, she thought the idea of women's rights was just and long overdue. Rose knew it was just something she was going to have to get used to. Along with everyone else in society if anything was going to change for women in the country.

"What is Helen going to do now?" Rose asked.

"She and Alexander will get married in the next few days. She said they will move to Kansas where they will take up his family's business. Printing or something or other." Siobhan shook her head. "I still think it was a big mistake to marry him. I don't think Helen loved him at all. She should have taken my advice."

"And done what?"

"She could have had an abortion."

And with that, Angelina did a quick sign of the cross and dropped her face into her hands, and Siobhan began to explain the procedure to Rose.

Rose could feel the warmth drain from her body as cool dampness covered her skin and she shivered in response. She gasped for air, pushed back her chair as she stood and the floor beneath her feet felt soft as the room began to move in a sideways direction. Rose stumbled backward as she tried in vain to grab hold of the table's edge to steady herself, but she could feel herself falling uncontrollably. And just before she blacked out Rose remembered feeling the faint touch of two arms lowering her to the ground.

23

Rose blinked away the fog as the distant voices calling her name grew closer and louder. The coolness she felt in her face was replaced with the warmth of a gentle repeated tap on the side of her face as her eyes came into focus. Standing above her were a crowd of faces, some calling her name and others watching with curiosity. Siobhan's red hair made it easy to recognize her place in the crowd, but it was the warmth of the voice speaking close to her ear that caught her attention.

"Peter!" Rose mumbled. "This is not how I wanted to tell you I was back."

Peter rubbed the top of Rose's head, and she realized he was holding a damp cloth on her forehead, "It's a good thing I was near."

Rose remembered the faint touch as she was falling, and realized it was Peter who lowered her to the ground saving her from a painful fall.

Thankfully Ms. Miller attributed Rose's fainting to her shock of returning to work so quickly and her concern over her father and insisted she lay down in the staff medical office and allow a nurse to tend to her for an hour or so. However, it took the nurse only twenty minutes and a glass of juice to put Rose right on her feet and return her to work with only her ego slightly bruised.

The end of the workday came, and Rose rushed to meet Peter outside the staff doors on the sidewalk, as she had done many times before, and they walked towards her apartment as they did before she left New York for Clarington.

Peter grabbed hold of Rose's hand and pulled her in close and kissed her cheek. A month ago, she would have tensed at the show of affection; however, today she grabbed Peter's elbow tightly and held her body next to his as they walked along the street.

The time they had been apart seemed to make each of them fonder of each other and they spent the following weeks enjoying every spare moment they had together. Every evening they walked from work taking the long walk home in place of the ride on the train car and they talked about everything relevant in their lives. They shared their pasts, their dreams, and planned their futures together.

While Rose was away in Clarington, Peter had searched and found a farm just outside of the city limits and collected some lavender from the field. He had been drying the plants and saving them for Rose so she could continue to make the soaps she loved so dearly, and that he grew to appreciate as well.

The day he gave Rose the saved flowers she carried them home as if they were a newborn baby. She placed them gently on her bed and unwrapped the package and breathed in a deep gulp of the aroma and closed her eyes. Joyful tears began to form in her eyes at the idea of Peter not only believing in her dream but caring enough to remember it so purely and perfectly.

A few weeks later Rose presented him with a special bar she made with his gift of lavender leaves once the batch had dried, "I added a little sage to it for you. To make it more masculine."

He held the bar in his hand and raised it to his nose and smiled, "Perfect. Just like you Rose."

Rose tilted her head down and leaned it against his shoulder. She was so happy she could cry. He gently shifted her body until they were facing each other and held her gaze with his eyes.

"We are perfect for each other Rose. You know that don't you."

She did and was so happy she was finally brave enough to admit it. Not only to herself but to her friends and especially to Peter.

It was the start of another work week and it had been raining hard all day until the moment Rose ran out of the hotel to meet Peter after work. The rain stopped, the clouds cleared, and the evening sun began to quickly warm the city. She was so full of emotion when she ran out the doors and saw his smiling face turned her way as he waited with his collar turned up under the cream-colored awning. She pushed her way through the doors and rushed into his arms and wrapped herself around his neck.

"I love you, Peter," Rose blurted out and took him completely by surprise but not shock, and he only wrapped his arms around her more tightly until he whispered in her ear, "I know."

But tonight, his voice had a different tone. Not a jovial, lighthearted tone he normally took with Rose. He was more serious and for the first time since Rose met Peter, he seemed nervous.

Rose placed her soft hand against his cheek where the stubble had begun to appear along the edge of his jaw, and she caressed his face and she answered as he did that time in the rain, "I know."

"I am serious Rose. We are perfect for each other and we are meant to be together. I want us to be together. Marry me, Rose!"

It was a statement more than a question, and one that Rose knew what her response was going to be without thinking about it.

She held his gaze with her eyes and his face in her hands as she nodded yes, and the tears spilled from the edge of her eyes.

Peter wrapped his arms around Rose and pulled her close and kissed her through the tears and the laughter.

He fumbled his hand into his pocket and pulled out a soft blue velvet box and held it in his shaking hand. Peter lowered himself to one knee and took Rose's left hand in his.

"Rose, I have loved you from the moment I met you, and I know that I will love you until I die, and if there is a heaven after that, I will love you there too," he pulled the shining ring from its box and slipped it onto Rose's finger. "Rose Farnsworth, will you marry me?"

"Yes! Yes! I will," Rose wrapped her arms around his neck and kissed him as they stood in the middle of the park and the few onlookers clapped in celebration.

Peter picked Rose up and twirled her around, "I can't believe you said yes! I can't wait to set the date that you will become Mrs. Peter Albert."

"Mrs. *Alberti*," Rose corrected him and then said, "How about this Saturday."

24

Rose wasted little time bursting out the news that she and Peter were engaged to be married. Joe took a liking to Peter immediately upon the first time they met, so it was no surprise that he was happy about the news of Rose's marriage and he eagerly agreed to give Rose away the following Saturday, seeing as he was her only relative that would be in attendance. There would be no need for flower girls or ring boys since Rose and Peter had agreed to a small, simple wedding. It was the one way they could guarantee being married on the following Saturday and without the guilt and stress of having her parents arrange a wedding Rose knew that they could never afford it. Siobhan and Angelina offered to help Rose search for the perfect dress once she told them she was going to 'piece something together' from the clothes she had.

"That is no way to start your life together Rose," Siobhan scolded. "Every bride needs a new dress to start a new life. Even if it just a simple, plain smock."

Angelina agreed and offered to stitch a simple veil from some lace as a gift to Rose. Ms. Miller even seemed to relax at the notion that they were planning to be married, holding intact the reputation of the hotel. Especially after the incident with Helen seemed to unsettle Ms. Miller for over a week. Peter's family offered to host the wedding reception at their restaurant and with Rose's family being uninvolved, she welcomed their offer.

"Well, I guess the only thing left to do is to plan your honeymoon," Siobhan winked.

"Peter and I decided we would spend the week getting our apartment ready. Maybe even sneak away to New Jersey for a night or two."

"That's a great idea Rose," Angelina said. Of her two close friends, Angelina was the most moved by the idea of falling in love and getting married. Siobhan teased that it was because of her Italian heritage that it was all she knew, but Rose felt it was something more than that. Angelina was a dreamer and always saw the brighter side of things no matter how hard things seemed to get. Whether it was at work or to do with things she was passionate about, Angelina always believed that if you dreamed big enough that everything would work out. Since Peter's proposal, Angelina used

Rose as an example of how things can work out if you try hard and stick to your beliefs.

"You never know what is right around the corner," Angelina would say. Believing that Rose and Peter's love was a sign of good things to come.

✳ ✳ ✳

Friday quickly came and Rose awoke earlier than her alarm buzzer rang, full of the excitement the day before a wedding brings. Rose had packed the few belongings she had on Tuesday and kept only her blue flowered dress laid out for today. Joe had prepared a full breakfast for him and Rose to share and admitted that he was going to be sad to lose her, and he called her his best roommate.

Joe had revealed his true feelings for Georgina over the last week and told Rose that he could see spending the rest of his life with her and having a family. He knew that there were obstacles to climb and that any marriage between two people of different color had many detractors who would want to stop them, but he was determined to be with the woman he loved. No matter what. Rose had inspired him, he said. To come to a city and not know a soul and carve out a life for herself and in the process to find true love. It was all it took to set Joe on his path. He planned on asking Georgina to marry him after Rose was married. He swore Rose to secrecy and then revealed his plan to whisk her away to New Jersey and propose on the boardwalk. He then pulled out the diamond he had already purchased as her engagement ring. It was three times the size of the one that Peter gave Rose, and she could only imagine how shocked Georgina would be and how beautiful it would look on her hand.

As on her first day in New York, Joe took Rose into the city and walked her to the hotel. "This is it Rose, your last day as a single working woman," he pulled his cousin close and gave her a warm hug. "Enjoy the attention Rose, you deserve it."

Joe watched from across the road as Rose walked towards the hotel staff entrance. When he recalled that moment later to Georgina, he said that he was sure there was a skip in her step as she walked along the side of the stone building and disappeared through the revolving doors knowing her future was bright.

* * *

The morning passed slowly and without much else but her wedding day on her mind. Rose glanced at the clock so frequently she started to annoy herself.

"Relax Rose," Siobhan said, "the time will go much more quickly if you are not watching the clock."

"I can't help it I...." The screeching of an alarm bell interrupted Rose as it echoed through the cavernous halls of the hotel. The deafening blare reverberated through the hotel shaking the single glass pane on the doors and windows.

"Fire?!" Angelina asked and shouted simultaneously.

Siobhan shook her head, "No, that's not the fire alarm. It's different."

They opened the door to the hall to investigate and watched the bodies of the other staff employees run down the hall and towards the side lobby exit. Not sure what they should do, they decided to follow the crowd and head towards the exit.

The lobby was filled with people. Staff and guests congregated together trying to figure out what the emergency was that summoned the screeching alarm through the building.

Siobhan grabbed the arm of the hotel manager as he was passing by and said, "What gives?"

When he turned to face Siobhan, the look of fear on his face told her it was something major that had happened. He mumbled something in response to Siobhan's question and when she shook him and asked him again. He repeated himself, this time in a louder voice. "There's been an accident."

"Where?" Siobhan asked.

The hotel manager held out his trembling hand and pointed towards the elevator bank. "I tried to grab him, he tripped and fell. I, I, just," the manager broke free of Siobhan's grasp and ran towards the offices behind the front reception desk area.

"Who fell?" Siobhan yelled after him.

The manager turned to face Siobhan and after a glance at Rose he returned Siobhan's gaze, "the bellhop."

The scream that came from Rose's lips was something primal and guttural that people had a difficult time describing later when they recalled the events of the afternoon. It was the kind of scream that only deep pain could illicit and that made you feel guilty hearing it and being present during such a profound personal tragedy.

Rose pushed her way past the crowd of bodies that stood between her and the bank of elevators. Onlookers were being held back by employees who showed a deep look of shock on their faces. They stood pale from the upset of the accident and some tried in vain to hold back their emotions as they announced that the area had to be kept clear.

One such employee was Ralph who while holding back two guests who were trying to see what had happened, caught Rose's eye as she steamrolled her way screaming towards where he stood. He released his grip on the two guests and grabbed hold of Rose's shoulders, "Don't Rose."

"Please tell me it's not Peter. Please, Ralph, tell me," Her pleading cries drew tears and cries from others who stood around her that knew of her love for Peter. And, of their plans for their wedding the next day.

Ralph shook his head and Rose watched his trembling lips as he whispered, "I am so sorry Rose."

Her fingers ran along Ralph's arms fitfully and she struggled to control them. Her legs folded under her body and she crumpled to the ground and came to rest at Ralph's feet. Her stomach tightened, her head swirled, and she felt as if she was going to be sick. Oh God, she prayed, don't let this happen, not again. Rose's world began to fold in on itself and the feeling she held earlier that day that her life was going to be perfect disappeared into the shouts and cries around her.

She lay at Ralph's feet sobbing and fighting the terrible feeling of loss and the frightening prospect of her life without Peter.

25

Two proposals and two dead fiancés. They were odds that even the unluckiest of girls never would have thought would have befallen her. Yet here was Rose huddled under her covers on the day that she was to be married to Peter faced with the prospect of laying another man she loved to rest. The ringing of the emergency alarm continued to echo in her head long after Joe had arrived at the hotel to take Rose home. Rose had laid on the hotel floor crying until the emergency crew arrived and lifted Peter from the bottom of the elevator bank. Siobhan and Angelina had tried, along with a sobbing Ralph, to get Rose to leave while they removed Peter from where he fell.

"No," Rose had insisted. "I want to be here when they bring him up."

Siobhan and Angelina wrapped their arms around Rose and held her tightly and together they waited, and watched, as three emergency-crew men carefully lifted Peter from the bottom of the elevator bank. They managed to shield Rose's view until the moment Peter's body was laid flat on the floor and covered carefully with a sheet.

Rose crawled over to where Peter lay, and she gently stroked his hair in place. Combing his hair to the left with her shaking fingers, just how he preferred to wear it. Everyone let her stay that way until she was ready to have him carried away. Siobhan made sure that the hotel manager contacted his family, to save Rose the pain of breaking the news to his mother.

There were numerous fatalities at workplaces such as theirs; however, somehow not many people spoke of them. Elevators, as it turned out, took many a life such as Peter's.

Rose later learned that Peter had summoned the elevator from the fifth floor where he was sent to help a room attendant bring a load of sheets and towels down to the laundry room. Peter, eager to see Rose, had not wanted to take two trips so he had balanced an extra load on the trolley he was pushing. When the elevator doors hissed open the elevator bank was devoid of a car. With sheets and towels piled high, Peter could not see the cavernous hole that was in front of him. He pushed the trolley forward and took a fateful step into the hole thinking there was the elevator car floor ahead. The hotel manager was standing behind him and when he saw the trolley car pitch sharply and fall, he reached out to grab Peter's coat but failed to grasp him tightly enough and Peter plummeted to his death.

It didn't matter to Rose how frequent these 'accidents' were. The emptiness and pain she felt deep in her stomach felt more like a betrayal of fate than an accident. It was a hollowness she knew would never be filled and she wondered how she was going to carry forward.

Rose didn't hear Joe open the door to her room, nor did she hear his steps along the floor as he walked beside her bed. It wasn't until he gently touched her shoulder that she even knew he was in the room.

"Rose," he whispered. "Why don't you get up and start to get ready. Georgina and I are going to take you to see Peter's parents now. We should get there before..."

Joe had a hard time admitting Peter was gone, and instead of the excitement of getting ready to give Rose away at her wedding, he was preparing for her fiancé's funeral.

Rose nodded and flung the cover off the bed and dragged her legs over the side and forced herself up. The stinging feeling of salt dried tears on the rim of her eyes ached with every blink. A heavy tightness radiated from the crown of her head to the base of her jaw making her dizzy with every move. Eventually Rose managed to stand and pull her grey wool dress past her aching neck. She slowly brushed out the curls in her hair and she felt an overwhelming urge to crawl back under the covers of her bed and hide away for the remainder of the day. But she knew that she couldn't do that. She owed Peter that much. She had to make the effort to honor the love they had and to be there for his parents. It is something she knew that he would have done for her.

When Rose walked out of her room Georgina quickly stepped towards her, tears in her eyes, and wrapped her arms securely around Rose. Rose stood like that, feeling the strength and friendship that she and Georgina had built over the months they knew each other and used it to summon the strength to try and face the day. And when she was ready, Rose nodded to them both that they should leave.

* * *

Joe and Georgina followed behind Rose as they approached Joe's family's restaurant. A small hand-printed sign was taped to the window. '*Closed due to a death in the family.*' Rose pretended not to see the sign on the window as they entered the restaurant. The day passed with Rose in a haze as she watched people hug each other and cry and approached her with more hugs and cries. She was grateful for the time with Peter's parents but was also grateful when the end of the day brought a respectable time to exit and return to the solace of her apartment with Joe and Georgina.

The weekend that held so much promise and excitement was quickly replaced with one of hopelessness and sadness. Rose unwrapped the dress that she had planned to marry Peter in and slipped it on. She slowly zipped the back of the dress closed and brushed her hands across the front of the light white dress feeling the soft silk that ran beneath her fingers. She reached down and lifted the finely stitched veil that Angelina made for her and placed it on the top of her head and let the lace fall against her soft curls.

She pulled the lace over her face and stared into the mirror. Even under the lace of the veil, Rose could see the face of a girl with no hope. The tears filled her eyes and spilled down the front of her cheeks. As they fell from her eyes Rose was resolved to never let her heart break again.

26

Three days seemed long enough to stay away from her real life. Once Rose had unpacked the belongings she had packed in preparation to start her life with Peter, she could see no reason to stay home. The apartment felt even more cramped with Joe's over attentiveness and preoccupation with trying to help Rose forget everything that happened. Joe meant well but Rose couldn't see how he could make her forget the man whom she was about to marry was killed. And she didn't see why she should.

Rose arrived at work a half-hour early and saw Ms. Miller walking towards the hotel entrance and dashed behind a newsstand to hide from her view. She may have been ready to leave the apartment and return to work, but she wasn't ready for the onslaught of sympathy chats she was bound to encounter. Especially ones from Ms. Miller.

Rose slipped into a boutique store that was located across the street from the hotel. She wandered the aisles busying herself by looking at various products on the shelves. In her attempt to avoid speaking with the shop keeper who was making his rounds to customers assisting them with their purchases, she grabbed a bottle and began to read the label closely. Once the coast was clear, she returned the bottle to the shelf and noticed sitting next to it was an assortment of soaps and bars. Rose lifted a nondescript packaged bar to her nose and inhaled the scent. Or lack thereof. One after the other the bars were devoid of smell and life, of any enjoyment. She thought back to the dried lavender that Peter collected and gave to her as a gift. The enjoyment he had when he opened the bar that she specially made for him. Rose returned the bars to the shelf and then realizing the time, made her way out of the store and across the street to the hotel.

She kept her head lowered and made her way down the long hall to the laundry room without being stopped by anyone. She pushed through the door to the laundry room and gave a quick nod to Siobhan and Angelina without slowing her step. She headed directly for the change room and once she was in her uniform she returned to the main room and began to work on a pile of laundry that was dumped in the back of the room. Instinctively her friends knew that Rose was not ready to talk, and just being around her friends was enough to comfort her for now.

The hours of the morning moved quietly and quickly until Siobhan placed her hand on Rose's shoulder and told her it was time for their lunch break. Rose walked in-between Siobhan and Angelina and together they protected her from invisible eyes and glances from fellow employees. It didn't take long to realize that Rose was safe from any outward signs of condolences or words of wisdom of 'how to carry on', as they sat unbothered while they ate their lunch. The conversation stayed focused dully on weather and fashion and then diverted to the latest celebrity to stay as a hotel guest.

"Martha Breborne," Siobhan said. "I think that is what her real name is or was."

"Are you sure?" Angelina asked.

"No. But it is something like that," Siobhan shrugged her shoulders. "It's Missy Marleigh now, and that is all anyone knows her as anyway."

"Except for her family," Angelina added.

"Yes, Angelina," Siobhan snickered. "Except for her family."

"Is she the one in the silent picture that we went to see together?" Rose asked. "It just came out."

Siobhan nodded, "She is here to do some PR stuff. Rumor has it that she is set to star in three movies this

219

year alone and the studio is gearing up to have her be their top-rated actress in their films."

"She is very glamourous," Rose agreed.

"And she came out of nowhere too," Siobhan said, and when Rose and Angelina looked confused, she added, "You know the story? Missy, or Martha, or whoever, came from nothing. She was the middle child of a farming family in Texas, five girls, I think. Anyhow, it was a studio executive who found her. He was driving through her small town when his car broke down. Her father was driving by and offered to help. He ended up spending the evening at their farm until a part could be brought in for his car and he was smitten with her immediately. They worked quickly and signed her and for the next six months, they fine-tuned her speech and got rid of her Texas accent, and taught her how to be comfortable around photographers and news people. The acting came naturally."

They continued talking about Missy Marleigh for the remainder of their lunch break. And for the rest of the afternoon, Siobhan and Angelina let Rose work in silence as they muddled through the next few hours of the day. The whole afternoon Rose replayed the story of Missy Marleigh and how she created a dream life out of a chance encounter. Rose also couldn't get Peter out of her mind and how he always said she would do something great.

When it was time to leave for the day, Rose quickly changed and ran from the laundry room, down the hall, and out the door, and then directly across the street. She pushed open the large glass door of the boutique store she sought refuge in earlier today before work, except this time she searched out the store owner.

"Excuse me," Rose nervously asked the man she thought was the owner.

He turned to face Rose and she was instantly put at ease with his warm relaxed smile that stretched across his cherubic face. His cheeks were spotted with a light blush from having just carried a load of heavy boxes from the storeroom. He placed the boxes on the ground and then brushed the dust from his hands on his white smock. He stood over six feet tall and when he straightened his back his round belly passed beyond the tip of his toes casting a shadow over Rose.

"How can I help you dear?" he asked.

"I was looking at your soaps earlier today, and, well, I noticed you just have plain soaps available."

"Yes. Well, what type of soaps would you expect to find?" he laughed.

Rose steadied herself, "Well, back home, I made soaps with flowers and herbs from the garden. Like lavender, and I was wondering if you would be interested in carrying them?"

The man, obviously taken aback by the proposal, crossed his arms, and squinted his eyes. "Are you working for some salesman?"

"No sir. I just thought if I was looking for something like that, maybe some of your other customers would be as well. And my friends who I make them for love them very much and think I should try selling them." An image of Peter flooded back into Rose's mind and she fought back the tears that threatened to come.

"I have to be honest, I never thought of it. And I never had a woman come in and try and sell me anything before either," He rubbed the stubble on his chin while he assessed Rose and mulled over her proposition. Then a smile crept across his face, "How about you bring me some of your soaps and we can see how they go over with the customers before I agree to take any on permanently?"

Rose shoved her hand towards the shop keeper and agreed. He laughed as he shook her hand and they planned to meet the next day.

Rose turned to leave the shop and as she made her way to the train a mixture of joy and sadness overcame her as tears began to cloud her eyes. She arrived at the platform and when the doors opened, she sat in the first empty seat she saw. The old man that sat across from Rose watched her as she settled in, and the look of profound sadness displayed in the downturned lines in his face. And in each other, they recognized the scar of a deep loss and the price for loving someone so deeply.

27

Rose held the package flat on her lap, careful not to get a rip in the brown wrap surrounding the bars of soap. Rose polished each bar and wrapped them with a thin brown string and attached a hand-printed tag to each bar. She stayed up past two in the morning working on each bar and package until she felt they were perfect. The scent of lavender rose from the package and calmed Rose as she traveled into the city on the train. Surrounded by morning travelers making their way to work, Rose felt a surge of purpose as she made her way to present her bars to the shop keeper who would hopefully put them on his shelf.

She arrived at the shop and pushed open the heavy glass door and walked to the back of the shop. Mr. Sterns was arranging jars on the top shelf of the preserve section and was easy to spot from the front of the store.

"Good morning Mr. Sterns," Rose cheerfully greeted him.

"Good morning dear," Mr. Sterns smiled as Rose approached him with the package of soaps. "And what do we have there?" he teased.

"Your next big seller, Mr. Sterns," Rose placed the wrapped package on the counter and gently pulled at a single string and loosened the bow. The thick brown paper fell to the counter revealing individually tagged bars of soap with flecks of lavender flowers, sage, and lemon balm. Each one emanating a deeply relaxing fragrance.

Mr. Sterns leaned his tall frame down until his face neared the counter and inhaled a deep breath, "These are astounding! And you say you make these? Yourself?"

Rose nodded, "Yes, sir. I have been making bars like these with my mother since I was a little girl."

"Very nice. Very nice indeed!" Mr. Sterns exclaimed.

"What is very nice?" A sharp, voice came from behind where Rose and Mr. Sterns stood. Rose turned and faced an older weathered woman who stood four inches shorter than Rose. What struck Rose immediately was that this was not a kindly older woman like you would think a grandmother to be. No. Instead, the woman who approached the counter did so with an acerbic gaze and a sagging frown. Her head was covered with coarse grey hairs tinged with yellow from years of smoking, and her thinning lips revealed a slice of worn teeth that refused to pass up a smile.

"This dear," Mr. Sterns passed one of the lavender bars to the old woman who was unmistakably his wife.

The worn Mrs. Sterns grabbed hold of the bar in her frail hands dotted with spots of age and rolled it around in her fingers before returning it to her husband's grasp.

"What do you think dear?" Mr. Sterns asked.

"About what?" Mrs. Sterns snapped.

"I am going to put these on the shelf and see how they go over with our customers. At the very least it will make the shop smell great," Mr. Sterns offered Rose a warm reassuring smile.

"No. It won't sell. These fad things never do." Mrs. Sterns snapped.

Rose held her breath and felt the tears rise in her eyes.

"But, dear," Mr. Sterns pleaded.

"We are going to stick to the products our customers have come to expect and that we know will sell. And that is that." Mrs. Sterns turned around and headed back to the storeroom from where she surfaced just a few moments earlier.

Mr. Sterns placed the lavender bar he held in his hands back on the pile of soap, "I am sorry dear. Maybe try in a few weeks?" he suggested.

Rose haphazardly wrapped the bars in the brown wrap, thanked Mr. Sterns, and turned to leave before the dejection overtook Rose.

Rose pushed her way to the front of the store, pulled open the heavy glass door, and stepped into the morning that earlier seemed so promising and full of hope. She dashed across the street, weaving around people making their way to work, and with her head pointed down, pushed through the revolving doors of the staff entrance at the back of the hotel.

In the staff room, Rose tossed the bars in the trash can sitting in the corner of the room. Afraid to ask herself what she was going to do next.

28

Because of the resounding turnout at her first live performance, Missy Marleigh had extended her stay at The Hotel Penn by an extra week. The number of people crowding the lobby grew each day. Some were curious guests hoping to catch a glimpse of the star as she made her way to and from her room, others, Ms. Miller was sure were photographers hoping to catch a shot of the glamourous star in an awkward pose or on the arm of a mysterious man. Such was the trend that was unfolding in the magazines.

Rose was glad for the overabundance of people crowding the hotel not because she looked forward to mingling with lots of people. On the contrary. She felt that it helped distract the staff of the hotel with the goings-on of Missy Marleigh and kept them from plying her with unwanted questions or swooning of condolences.

Rose wiggled her way into the back of the overcrowded laundry room and busied herself with the large piles of towels and sheets that were being dumped in her path. Extra guests for the hotel meant extra work for the laundry staff, for which, Rose was happy for the mindless distraction. It was helping take her mind off Peter as well as the morning's dejection by Mr. Sterns.

"Miss Farnsworth," Ms. Miller stood at the entrance of the laundry room, one hand on her hip and the other propping open the door as she yelled across the room.

Rose turned and saw Ms. Miller extend her slim finger and crank it towards where she was standing, silently summoning her from across the room.

"Yes Ms. Miller," Rose said when she was close enough to speak in a quiet voice.

Ms. Miller nodded her head towards the empty hall and turned around and began to walk down the long corridor. Rose quietly followed. They walked in silence until they reached the main floor.

"Take these up to the seventeenth floor," Ms. Miller pushed a cart towards Rose and handed her a ring of keys. "These are special gifts from the hotel for Missy Marleigh and her entourage." Miss Miller rolled her eyes towards the crowd in the lobby. "Please see that they are arranged in each room appropriately."

"Don't you think a chambermaid would do a better job?" Rose asked remembering when Ms. Miller reprimanded her for her inadequate job the last time she filled in for the duties of a chambermaid.

Ms. Miller answered as she walked away, "No, I don't"

"But why me?" Rose called after her.

Ms. Miller stopped, turned her head over her shoulder, and looked at Rose, "You are the only one without her head in the clouds these days Rose."

Rose stood shocked and had even thought she saw a slight smile cross Ms. Miller's face. The closest she was surely ever going to come to a compliment from Ms. Miller.

Rose fingered through the assortment of specialty items arranged on the cart. They were in no particular order and included sweets wrapped in gold foil from a confectioner in New Jersey, handmade chocolates poured by the head chef at the five-star resort that just opened in upstate New York, and several other items that fashioned themselves more as gifts than typical room accoutrements.

Rose slipped the keyring into her pocket and began to push the cart towards the elevators. The clamoring of bodies and tapping of the leather souls of shoes echoed in the open lobby area to the left of where Rose stood. She waited behind the large marble column pillar until the crowd passed by.

"Miss Marleigh! Miss Marleigh!" shouts from reporters and fans echoed towards a group of ten people that had just exited an elevator.

The footsteps stopped and a soft voice echoed over the dinging of the elevator bells, "Yes, dear." It struck Rose how mature her voice sounded for such a young person. Then she remembered Siobhan telling her how the movie executives groomed Missy.

"Your fans want to know Missy, what is your secret to success?" it was a reporter Rose recognized from the New York fashion magazine, although she couldn't recall his name, she recognized him by his byline photo.

"Secret? Darling, just good 'ole fashioned hard work."

Then another reporter took an opportunity and shouted out another question, "What do you miss most about home Miss Marleigh?"

The crowd stood silent as Missy thought about her answer to a question that seemed to take her by surprise, "Well, I would have to say the smell of the field flowers behind our home. Especially at this time of year, they would be in full bloom by now."

"Not like the streets of New York?" a wisecracking reporter shouted into the crowd, and elicited a peal of rousing laughter, saving Missy Marleigh from the awkwardness of responding.

As Missy and her entourage made their way to the front doors of the hotel, the throngs of reporters and fans followed along in hopes of their chance at getting one more glimpse, photograph, or question before she disappeared into the waiting limo.

When the lobby had quieted, Rose began to push the cart towards the elevator then suddenly stopped as a thought occurred to her. She swerved the cart and headed back towards the laundry room. She ran by the others working at the folding tables and into the staff room and directly towards the trash can in the corner of the room. She hoped that no one had dropped anything wet that would have soiled her package in the last few hours and cursed herself for her rashness in throwing out the soaps she worked so hard at creating. Salvaging a few bars, she ran back to the cart and quickly made her way up to the seventeenth floor.

Rose ran her finger down the hotel guest manifest that was attached to the clipboard on the cart until she found Missy Marleigh's name and when she found it, she ran her finger across to the far right of the page to locate her room first. Rose made her way to room 1783 and slipped the master key into the lock and turned the handle of the door. She pushed the cart inside and looked around.

It was this same room that she had been in at the beginning of her employment at the hotel and saw exquisite clothes and shoes and magazines and thought she could never see anything that could compare. Until today.

Rose walked into the bathroom and replaced the bathrobe with an even more plush robe that had MM embroidered in gold thread on the chest pocket. She placed shampoo from London, and a bottle of the latest perfume from Paris to hit the market, on the glass shelf above the sink.

Rose then pulled out a bar of soap from her pocket and was struck by the scent of lavender that filled the room. She removed the plain bar that rested on the glass soap dish and placed her handmade bar with purple flecks in its place, complete with the string and tag in place. One that she had stayed up until two in the morning to complete and it looked perfect.

When Rose was finished, she continued to the remaining rooms on her list and within an hour she was done. She returned the cart to the main floor and resumed her place at the folding table. This time with a relaxed grin on her face.

* * *

"Miss Farnsworth!" Miss Miller's kind approach earlier that morning had been replaced by a stern reprimanding tone that shook those around the room.

The color faded from Rose's face as she turned around. Stares of shock covered the faces of everyone working in the room with Rose and now worked fitfully to not make eye contact with either Rose or Ms. Miller.

"Yes Ms. Miller," Rose answered.

"Come with me."

The door slammed as Ms. Miller had already departed the room and was stomping her feet towards her office. Rose ran from the room and sprinted to catch up to Ms. Miller.

Hearing her footsteps, Ms. Miller pivoted on her toes, "Just one thing I asked you. One! I was giving you a chance. With everything you had been through, I thought you deserved it. Now you made us both look like fools."

"What is wrong? What did I do?"

"Missy Marleigh is at the front desk now looking to speak with Mr. Statler because of something that was left in her room."

Without speaking further, Ms. Miller resumed her stride towards the lobby and then into the back room where Missy Marleigh stood holding the lavender bar of soap in her left hand as she was speaking with Mr. Statler. As Rose walked closer, she noticed Missy's cheeks were flushed red and damp with tears that flowed from her eyes. Although she could not hear their words, Rose could tell the conversation they were having was animated.

"Mr. Statler. Miss Marleigh. I do apologize on behalf of the hotel," her hands were grasped together so tightly that the white of her knuckles threatened to pop from her skin. "I have brought the employee here to apologize to Miss Marleigh directly. She will then be collecting her things and leaving the hotel."

Missy Marleigh turned to face Rose, and that is when Rose noticed the tears of rage were tears of joy as a soft smile crossed her face. She held the bar up, "Did you place this in my room?"

Rose nodded, "Yes ma'am."

"Where did you get this dear?"

Rose looked at Ms. Miller who wore a look of shock and then to Mr. Statler who was more curious as to her answer, "I made it."

Missy's eyebrows raised and she turned to face Mr. Statler, "You have a gold mine here. You are going to want to take advantage of this."

She then turned to Rose and placed her manicured and jeweled hand on her shoulder, "Thank you, dear, it was the most special surprise to walk into my room and smell this. It made me feel right at home."

Missy Marleigh thanked Mr. Statler and then excused herself so she could rejoin the crowd that awaited her in the lobby.

Ms. Miller's stern gaze was pointed directly at Rose; however, with Mr. Statler standing a few inches away smiling proudly at Rose, she could no sooner reprimand her than she could reprimand Mr. Statler. And Rose knew that Ms. Miller was wondering how Rose was able to avoid, once again, being sacked.

Mr. Statler thanked Ms. Miller for her help and put his arm around Rose's shoulder turning her towards a more private corner of the lobby, excluding Ms. Miller from any further point of their conversation.

Mr. Statler turned to Rose and asked her one simple question. And as he waited for an answer to that question, the moment hung tensely suspended between them, waiting for the word that would allow Rose to decide in which direction it would take her life.

29

With the season's change into autumn, and then winter, there also were profound changes coming to the city. There had been, over many years, a movement of temperance that was pushing the city and the country into a state-regulated law of alcohol restriction. The time would come to be known as Prohibition, and although it would only last until 1933, those living in January 1920 had the impression it was a permanent change and direction for the country. Closer to home, the effect on Joe was disastrous to his already tenuous business venture.

Joe's special blend of gin with a higher alcohol content by now was fighting an already strictly regulated industry and had forced him to distribute to club owners outside the law and at much peril to himself and his business associates. When competitors either tried to muscle him out of business in the city or policemen would try and elicit bribes for offers of protection and promises of turning a blind eye – he had ended up robbed or beaten.

The push towards Prohibition had also seen the installation of a designated force of government agents whose sole job was to crack down on all illegal alcohol sales and manufacturing. Joe had felt he was forced to make the difficult decision to leave New York and relocate to Canada where he was able to produce and build his Beman Brooklyn Gin company with his special recipe and trademarked logo. It was also a chance for he and Georgina to get married and start their life together. Together, with Billy's blessing, they packed up their belongings in the dark blue truck he normally used to transport his gin, and they headed to Detroit where they would cross into Canada and begin their new life.

Rose nervously accepted the news knowing it was the push to further independence she needed, and the freedom and acceptance Joe deserved.

"You have to promise to come to visit," Joe told Rose.

Rose nodded, too full of emotion to speak and with tears filling her eyes she choked back her sobs and grabbed hold of Joe and hugged him as tightly as she could. He was her protector and guide when she began her new life in New York and now she was losing him. The loss; however, was made easier by the look of joy on both his and Georgina's face as they planned their escape.

Rose stood shivering on the bottom step of the building as Joe packed the last of their bags into the truck and pulled away from the curb and drove north towards his new life. She waited until he was out of sight and then turned around, headed up the stairs to the apartment, and closed the door.

She surveyed the apartment and even though Joe left the furniture, it seemed empty somehow just with the knowledge that he would not be returning. Timing; however, was also fortuitous as Angelina was ready to spread her wings and begin a term at the university preparing her studies in education. She convinced her parents to let her live with Rose where she could study and be closer to work on weekends. Somehow, miraculously her parents agreed to the plan. It took some convincing and a whole lot of guilt from her brother Sam who was preparing a big change in his life as well.

Sam had done what everyone thought was the impossible, he had convinced Siobhan to marry him. Angelina's parents were so excited (because for them a marriage brought the prospect of grandchildren) that they were easier to convince that Angelina's education was the best choice for her. Sam and Siobhan quickly planned a wedding and it promised to be an incredible event. Combining the exuberance and culture of both an Italian family and an Irish family proved to be just the thing everyone needed in this great time of change. And, as it turned out, just under the mark of the laws of Prohibition commencing.

Rose shivered, still cold from standing on the steps outside as Joe and Georgina departed under the steely grey sky that threatened the first snow of the season. Rose looked out the window of the apartment as the first few flakes of snow trickled from the sky landing on the ledge outside the window.

She noticed a folded piece of paper rested against an empty glass in the center of the table with Rose's name penned in Joe's messy scrawl. Rose wiped the trail of tears from her cheeks then grabbed the note from the table.

"Rose,

I know you are nervous about beginning this next stage of your life, but you must remember you are not <u>alone</u>. You were brave to come to New York when you were only seventeen and did not know a soul. You worked hard, had your heart break miserably and you are still standing!

Just remember to not be afraid to take chances.

Love, your cousin Joe

P.S. fill the glass with the bottle (you know where it is)"

Rose placed the note on the table and walked over to the cabinet under the sink where a bottle of Joe's special blend gin lay hidden behind a loose panel on the wall. She tugged at the trim, loosened the wood, and pulled out a full bottle of Joe's special gift. She tipped the bottle and filled the small glass to the rim.

Today Rose felt like she was reborn, just like the day she first arrived in New York. And now she was here, in her little apartment in Brooklyn where she was going to emerge as the person she was meant to be. She raised the glass to the skyline and in memory of the great loves of her life, took a slow swallow and let the burning liquid slowly sink in her body, warming her as it settled.

The journey of people through her life, even those along for a short ride, bequeathed memories largely of pain, seldom solely of joy, but had always managed to leave a lasting mark of love. Even though Rose was not able to control the events of her life, she was able to choose who she rode with. And for that, she felt blessed.

All of New York was filled with the same kind of people. Each with a different past, different hometowns, and a different history, but it was their dream for their future that brought them together and made them alike.

It was never clearer to Rose, as it was now when she stood in her small apartment and watched the darkened sky slowly settle over the city's skyline and knew that everyone gathered underneath it was in this together.

30

New York City, May 10th, 1993

The announcement caused more of an uproar than Andrew had anticipated. It was apparent ten minutes into the meeting that tradition and historical significance were important to only one person present that day, and Norman Martindale was unsuccessful in commanding an overwhelming sense of influence in the room.

Outside, the storm continued to batter the side of the building and now a blinding flow of water cascading over the outer shield of the window threatened to break through at any moment. The sound of the rain intensified as the wind increased to eighty miles an hour, challenging the strength of the frame. Thunder rumbled high above The Hotel Pennsylvania and shook the thin single pane glass, held flimsy in their frames with each explosion.

Andrew wrapped his hand around the edge of the podium and closed his eyes and listened to the numerous cries of discontent that rose from the crowd assembled in the room.

The financiers, along with Ben, stood shocked and shaking their heads at the back of the room. Each one with their arms folded tight in front of their chests stood dazed and wondered how one of their own could turn on them. Andrew was prepared for the onslaught of discontent from his business associates after he made the announcement. What he wasn't prepared for was the feeling of a fight that began to rise in him with each shout of discord as he began to reveal his plan. The whole plan.

As he spoke, he began to see the importance of the task thrust upon him and the impact it could have on the city. And with more resolve, he proceeded to defend his proposal.

"Mr. Ponetti, are you to tell us that you want to purchase the hotel?" Norman asked.

"Yes."

"And you intend to leave it operating as a hotel?" Norman tilted his head to the right and squinted one eye, as he asked in disbelief. He had never imagined a proposal such as this would be possible for the hotel.

"Yes. Exactly in the manner that Mr. Statler had intended. He had a vision for not only the hotel but the city. And I think it can work again. So many people built their lives around this hotel and Statler was instrumental in setting the tone and change for hotels and resorts around the world."

"So, nothing is going to change?" Ben shouted from the back of the room in a form of mild protest.

"Oh, a lot is going to change Ben. A lot." You're just not going to make a commission from it, Andrew thought.

Andrew began to briefly outline his plans to refurbish the hotel and restore the rooms and facilities to their original glory, respecting the vision of the original owner.

When asked why he would take such a financial risk, he just smiled. And without answering any further questions, he retrieved his coat and excused himself from the room. As he was leaving, he handed his card to Norman Martindale and told him he would be in touch.

As Andrew walked down the hall towards the lobby, he could hear Norman bang his gavel and happily call the meeting to a close.

* * *

Her thin hand, marked with eighty-one years of age, steadily reached out to press the button that quickly summoned the elevator to the ground floor. She held the room key tightly in her right hand and ran her thumb across the imprinted numbers on the tag. It was much quieter in the lobby than Rose had remembered; however, it had been a long time since she had been here, and her memory was getting more selective with the passing of time. She also seemed to think it was colder than before too, feeling the chill from the emptiness of the lobby run through her. When she first arrived in New York in 1919, there was an electrifying buzz in the air that had seemed to have fizzled over the years. Tears formed in her eyes as she thought of all the people she worked with at the hotel and her friends, all long passed, and how saddened they would have become at the current state of the hotel.

After Helen came to terms with the realization she was going to have the baby, she and Alexander married, moved to Kansas and together they had three more children. All sons. Helen quickly became instrumental in organizing a small business cooperative for women in the area. Women who had a fire in them as Helen did, and were lucky enough to have forward-thinking husbands at that time that supported their ventures. They were able to weather the storm of the impending depression that saw many of their husbands' businesses close.

Siobhan and Sam succeeded in having the most interesting wedding, blending Irish and Italian traditions into their modern ceremony, and for many was the last big splurge before Prohibition hit the city. Of course, Siobhan was able to hold off the arrival of children until she was ready for them to come into their lives. And when they were ready, they had one boy and one girl that they raised above the restaurant that they ran together until their son Albert took it over. Rose last saw her friend when she and Sam retired to Florida in 1978.

Angelina successfully obtained her Ph.D. in education and became a strong figurehead in the department of education. First for the state, then for the country. By the time Angelina retired at age seventy, she was responsible for passing over one hundred and twenty bills that enacted change that would benefit children across the country and give everyone equal access to quality education.

Joe and Georgina eventually settled in Windsor Ontario and together built Joe's specialty gin company while raising their family of five. Georgina never stopped singing, although her performances in clubs never reached the height it did while she was at Billy's. Rose and Joe never went very long without a visit and remained close until his death four years ago.

Most surprisingly Rose had learned that Ms. Miller had not always projected a sour disposition. It was at her funeral many years after Rose left the hotel that she met several children that Ms. Miller volunteered with at the city's orphanage. Many of the children lost their parents to illness, but it was the ones who lost their parents to the devastation of war that first attracted Ms. Miller to her clandestine work at the orphanage. It was at the orphanage where she spent her time when she was not working at the hotel. Rose learned that Ms. Miller had lost the love of her life during WWI when he was killed in action and was never able to move past her heartbreak. She donated most of her salary as well as her time to reading and tending to the children's emotional upbringing until the time they were either placed in homes or they reached the age they were able to leave the orphanage and begin their life. Each child had a different story, but all had the same memory of Ms. Miller, and that said owed all their success to her.

Rose was the last one alive but somehow felt closer to her friends just by being present in the hotel.

Why had she not come sooner, she wondered?

Although spring was usually a time of warmth in the city, the storm that hovered over New York for the last week began to settle a chill in everyone, and Rose shivered under her tan wool shawl. She watched the numbers above the brass elevator doors and waited as the light illuminated each passing floor as the car gradually descended towards the lobby where she stood waiting. She was alone as she waited for the brass doors to open and was thankful for the moment of privacy.

Especially today.

The chime rang as the elevator arrived on the main floor and the doors slid open with a hiss. She stepped onto the elevator and pressed the button that would carry her to the seventeenth floor. When the elevator doors closed, Rose became aware of the annoying tunes that echoed through the tiny speakers. Musak, Rose thought they called it. Rose chuckled as she wondered what someone like Mickey Hughes would have thought of the jingle that swirled around her now. Not much, she imagined.

When they reached the seventeenth floor the doors slid open and Rose stepped into the hall. A feeling of excitement swelled as she approached room 1783. The servidors were long since out of use however they were still installed on the doors, even though they were painted and locked shut. It gave a charming reminder of a time when service to guests was at the forefront of the hotel.

Rose slipped the key in the lock and after a short turn and a click, she twisted the handle and pushed open the door.

The furniture had changed since she was last here in 1919 but the placement remained the same. Time was not kind to the paint or carpet and the bathroom, like the rest of the hotel, was in much need of upgrades.

Rose lay her purse on the end of the bed and slowly unzipped it, her hand shaking with age. She reached inside and removed a small package wrapped in her company's telltale brown wrap. It was a package that graced exclusive boutiques around the world and had become a familiar brand in many top resorts around the country. Rose raised the small package to her nose and breathed in deeply. The scent of lavender was a welcome aroma to the musty room.

Rose stepped into the bathroom and slowly unwrapped the paper and dropped the small square bar of soap into the palm of her hand. She removed the unsightly plain sliver of soap that was wrapped in a plastic seal sitting on the glass dish and replaced it with the lavender bar she removed from her purse.

Rose took a few extra moments to reminisce about the last time she left a bar just like this one in this room in 1919, and how it changed her life.

Mr. Statler could have fired her for those actions; instead, he took a keen interest in her idea. Fueled by his passion for the hotel and his comradery with Rose who was also from his home state of Ohio, he proposed a business venture, and together they formed the Farnsworth Soap Company. Initially Rose supplied The Hotel Penn with her specialty soap products; however, it didn't take long for word to spread and Rose's soaps were in huge demand. Mr. Statler introduced Rose to other hotel owners with the agreement that she would continue to supply his hotels first, and then he released his ownership of the company back to her where she built an international brand and a financial empire.

Rose was now able to be able to give back to the hotel that gave her a chance. A chance of a new life and where she found love.

Mr. Statler had sent Rose to work with his business apprentice Mr. Frank Ponetti, so she could learn the processes and formalities of establishing a brand that could be used in the hotel. Frank would recall that it was love at first sight. Rose; however, struggled to accept his attention and ignored her feelings, fearing that if she were to fall in love again it would only end in misery.

However, Frank was patient and waited until Rose was ready. And when she was, he took the train to Clarington, asked her father for her hand in marriage. Together they returned to New York as complete partners to build their life and the business that would support their family of five and thousands of employees that would come to work for The Farnsworth Soap Company.

Rose's looked back on her life and admitted it was blessed with tragedies that built her strength and character and opened her life to a love so strong that the harshness of living could never shake. Frank died in Rose's arms earlier that year and as he took his last breath it was on the end of his pledge to Rose, "I'll wait for you."

As they did in their life together, Rose and Frank also had a plan for the hotel, and today Rose and Andrew were here to see it come to fruition.

As Rose turned to leave, an overwhelming sense of purpose was fulfilled.

The fragrance of lavender began to fill the room and substitute the years of neglect with one of hope for the future. Rose retrieved her purse from the bed, left a sizable tip for the chambermaid, and prepared to leave the room.

For a fleeting moment, Rose was seventeen and full of hope, promise, and excitement. Innocence. Hope. Fear. Anticipation. Love. A myriad of emotions enveloped her as she surveyed the room that changed her life.

The rain was beginning to subside, and streams of light filtered through the drops of water that dotted the window and it slowly began to warm the room. Rose glanced at her watch and noticed it was time to leave. Her grandson Andrew would be done by now and waiting for her in the lobby.

Rose clung to the memories and scent of lavender that writhed entwined in the air as she glanced around the room, and contentment washed over this final stage of her life as she gently closed the door to room 1783.

The End

Author's Note

Thank you for reading, and I sincerely hope you enjoyed *The Hotel Penn*. As an independently published author, I rely on you, the reader, to spread the word. So, if you enjoyed the book, please tell your friends and family, and if it isn't too much trouble, I would appreciate a brief review.
Thanks again.
My best to you and yours.
L.L. Abbott

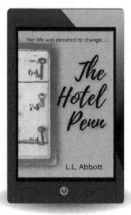
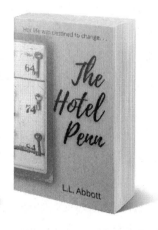

Hardcover, Paperback, eBook and Large Print editions

A little bit about The Hotel Penn . . .

On January 25, 1919, The Hotel Pennsylvania opened its doors to its first guests. The Hotel Pennsylvania was built by the Pennsylvania Railroad and operated by Ellsworth Statler and is situated across the street from Pennsylvania Station, known to commuters in New York as Penn Station.

Some details such as the name of the hotel, date of operation, and operating owner of The Hotel Pennsylvania are true. The Café Rouge was, in fact, the main restaurant in The Hotel Pennsylvania and did serve as a nightclub for many years. Puglia is indeed a fabulous restaurant in New York that was established in 1919, the same year as The Hotel Pennsylvania, which is why I felt it was important to be included in the novel.

Ellsworth M. Statler was a pioneer in the hotel industry and later in life was an integral part of The Hotel School at Cornell University. His depiction in this story is done in a light that favorably reflects his achievements and has him appear only as a subtle (but positive) character. The character of Eileen is also inspired by the real-life figure of Mary Eileen Bulman Abbott, a Canadian academic and community activist born in Winnipeg, Manitoba. Among many achievements throughout her life, she also attended Columbia University for advanced studies and was the first female president of the University of Manitoba Students Association, a great achievement that has made her family proud.

This, however, is where my imagination takes over and characters were shaped to allow the re-creation of important events that took place during 1919 in New York City. I wanted to create an emotional attachment to Rose Farnsworth, who at the age of seventeen ventures to step into a changing culture bravely crossing the chasm that separates her past from her future and her generation from the one before.

As Rose's life moves forward, she learns to adapt to the changing social and economic scene sweeping the country and reminds us all that change can be hard, but the rewards are often worth the effort.

This story is inspired by a vacation at The Hotel Pennsylvania in 2019, during their 100th anniversary. As I stepped off the elevator and onto the seventeenth floor I was immediately flooded with ideas for the characters in *The Hotel Penn*. Room 1783 showed me the city through the eyes of a fictional Rose Farnsworth and as I toured with my family I dreamed of what may have happened during that first year of the hotel's operation.

Thank you for stepping back in time and experiencing 1919 in New York City.

Other Books Available by L.L. Abbott

Mystery Series

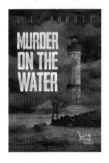 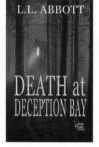 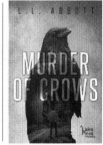 

  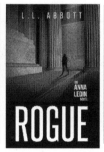 

 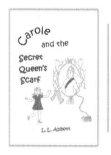